A Game of Brides

A Game of Brides

MEGAN CRANE

TULE
PUBLISHING

Chapter One

S HE FELT HIM before she saw him.

It was the same as it had always been during those long, golden Montana summers when she'd been unable to escape how helpless and wild he'd made her feel as an inexperienced teenager—that little shiver down the back of her neck, then snaking along her arms, as if every hair on her body was shivering to attention.

And then, because she wasn't a teenager any longer, lower. Much lower.

Emmy Mathis scowled at the baggage carousel at the Bozeman, Montana airport, willing her reaction away. Willing her goose bumps to disappear. Willing herself to feel none of that shimmering, infuriating *need* that curled like light deep inside her. Willing her absurd reaction to be nothing more than a response to the colder temperature.

It was May in Montana and only chilly for Emmy because she'd woken up this morning back home in much warmer Atlanta, and when she slung her duffel bag over her shoulder and turned around, he was there. Of course he was.

Standing by the wall, those unfairly gorgeous green eyes fixed on her in that brooding, knowing way of his. Just like any given day in any summer of her youth.

Especially that last summer. When she'd been eighteen and head over heels in love with him and he'd been completely out of her league—until that very last night before she'd left for college.

Her scowl deepened. And Griffin Hyatt—the bane of her existence and one of the ten million reasons Emmy wanted to be anywhere but back in Montana, even if that meant missing her only sister's wedding—grinned back at her.

If that was what that little crook of his hard mouth was.

He was whole lot older now than he'd been during those long ago summers. A grown man made entirely of smooth, lean, perfect muscle packed into faded jeans and an MSU T-shirt, with intricate tattoos peeking out from beneath each sleeve and all the way down the length of one corded, masculine forearm. His ridiculous green eyes packed the same hard punch she'd never quite managed to forget, and she wasn't in any way emotionally prepared for the way his too-long dark hair and that *mouth* of his hit at her, making her whole body feel too warm. Feverish, even. He was the kind of man who left scars. He had.

It was so unfair. If anyone deserved to turn ugly with age it was Griffin. Emmy wanted to dump her coffee on him in retaliation for any one of a thousand old sins—and maybe mess up some of his arrogant, lazy hotness as he stood there, studying her reaction with an intensity that made her stomach curl in on itself. It took every last shred of willpower she had to restrain herself.

This was merely an unfortunate coincidence, she assured herself. A chance encounter, nothing more. A mature person would smile, maybe even nod politely to an old acquaintance, so that was what Emmy did. And then she pretended he wasn't there as she looked away from him, gazing around for a member of her family, one of whom had been supposed to meet her plane this afternoon.

The same way she was pretending she'd never been naked in front of him—the way she'd *been* pretending for going on ten years now.

The baggage carousel emptied. The crowd dissipated. Emmy checked her phone approximately twelve thousand times, but there were still no messages from her parents or her sister to explain their absence.

It wasn't until the carousel had stopped moving and Emmy was the only one still standing there next to it that a hideous possibility occurred to her.

She tensed. She knew.

Then she turned slightly, stiffly, to find Griffin exactly where she'd last seen him. Leaning back against the wall, his arms folded over his lean, hard chest and his booted feet crossed, watching her like she was the most entertaining thing he'd seen in years.

Given what she knew about him through the family grapevine that he was a part of because their grandmothers— Gran Harriet and Gran Martha—were still the best friends they'd been when they'd roomed together at Radcliffe way back when, Emmy doubted very much that she entertained him even a little bit. She was a perfectly decent advertising copywriter who lived a perfectly nice life in perfectly comfortable Atlanta. Griffin was an extreme sports nut and athletic clothing entrepreneur who liked to fling himself down mountains and out of planes, making money and risking almost certain death every time he inhaled.

He'd been out of her league when she'd been eighteen. He was beyond her understanding now. But no less gorgeous, she couldn't help but notice. And even more compelling than he'd been back then.

Griffin lifted his upper hand with the same deceptively languid arrogance he apparently still did everything else and then crooked the top two fingers. Ordering her to come to him without uttering a single word.

Every last part of Emmy protested. Violently. Because there was too much of her that simply wanted to rush to obey him, the way she'd done more than she liked to admit to herself as a girl. And look where that had gotten her. Naked and abandoned the night before she'd left for college, and nary a word to or from this man since.

But there was no one else there who could possibly be her ride, and so she found herself walking toward him.

Reluctantly. She stopped when she was a foot or so away, and told herself her spiking body temperature had nothing to do with the frank, male appraisal in those green eyes of his as they ran over her, much less the way that mouth of his kicked up in one corner.

She wished, with a sudden onslaught of deep fervor, that she'd dressed up to travel today, the way her mother still did. She wished she'd done something with her hair besides clip it back out of her way with that ruthless efficiency her far more feminine and sultry sister Margery liked to call her *depressing practicality*. She wished she did the kinds of things to *her* jeans that Griffin did so effortlessly to his. That she was as ordinary as ever next to all his beaming male glory poked at her. It stung in old wounds she'd imagined long since healed. Emmy tucked her chin down toward the lightweight blue scarf she'd looped around her neck and glared at him.

"Hey, Bug," Griffin said. *Drawled,* really.

"Funny thing about the name Bug," Emmy replied, which was hard, given how tightly she'd clenched her teeth together at the sound of the nickname he'd given her when she was all of seven. "It's been ten years since anyone called me that and I still hate it. If you've forgotten my actual name, just say so."

The girl she'd been, awkward and emotional and *distraught* at the way this beautiful older boy looked right through her—until the summer he hadn't, bristled when he studied her for a long moment. She told herself she didn't flush. More, that she didn't remember his hands against her skin in the dark of his grandmother's barn. That she couldn't still taste him the way she had the last night she'd seen him.

"I know your name," he said.

"Then I have a great idea. Use it."

"Nice to see you too, *Emmy*," Griffin said, with that lurking hint of laughter and a completely unearned note of authority that put her back up. "You might want to mind your manners. I'm your ride."

"Why?" She made no effort to keep from glaring at him. Maybe that would hide all the rest of the things that swamped her then at the idea of being alone with him in a confined space. Or at all. "Did my entire extended family die from wedding overkill already? Or have you opened up a taxi service?"

"I'm not sure rural Montana is really the optimal place to launch a new taxi service," he said in his lazy way that still managed to remind her that he was the one who'd been written up in *Forbes* magazine, not her. "Way to think outside the box, though. I appreciate a new business proposition as much as the next guy."

"Why you?" She realized how rude that sounded when his dark brows rose over that dangerous gleam of amusement in his gaze, and she forced the kind of smile she used on her awful, patronizing boss. "I mean, surely you have better things to do. Don't you? Aren't you some kind of mogul these days?"

He smirked, she smiled harder, and Emmy was pretty sure both of them knew perfectly well that she knew exactly what he did. Or had done. GriffinFlight, his brand and ever-evolving product line, was turning up on every snowboarder, skateboarder, free-range skier, and surfer anyone had ever heard of lately. *Outside* magazine had called the tattoo-reminiscent designs "high-octane, a necessary blast of fresh air, and, in a word, hot."

Not that Emmy had ever Googled him.

"Something like that," Griffin said, with that knowing look on his face that Emmy felt everywhere. The way she always had.

"And yet you take time out of your busy *Wolf of Wall Street* day to play cab driver for me," she said, still smiling, though she made no attempt to keep that dry note from her voice. "I feel like Cinderella on her way to the ball. Which I believe makes you the pumpkin. Or a mouse pretending to be a man. Something like that, right?"

Griffin straightened from the wall then, and Emmy couldn't believe she'd forgotten how *tall* he was. Or maybe it was that he'd filled out in the decade since she'd last seen him, all that lanky restlessness she remembered turned into visible, unmistakable strength and power. Her throat went dry, and she hated herself.

"You haven't been here in a while," he said, low and per-fectly courteous, so there was no reason at all that Emmy should feel it wash through her like that. Like a wave of pure, hot, aching sensation, with a little bit of warning besides. "So maybe I need to remind you that our grandmothers deliberately bought adjoining land in the hills outside of Marietta so they could see each other all the time. We grew up here." He smiled at her, though there was that sharpness she remembered too well there, too, making it an edgy, challenging thing. *That* was the Griffin she knew, the Griffin she'd always wanted far more than was safe. Or wise. *Or requited,* a little voice reminded her. "Well. You were just a summer girl."

"Don't revise history I can remember all by myself," she chided him, shifting her duffel bag higher on her shoulder and tipping her chin up, like she was ready to go a few rounds with him. She thought maybe she was. The eighteen-year-old he'd abandoned so cavalierly deserved it. "You grew up in Baltimore. You went to one of those fancy New England prep schools. You lived in Marietta for exactly one semester before you went to Dartmouth."

"Glad to see you were paying such close attention," he murmured, a gleam she definitely didn't like in his eyes, and Emmy couldn't believe this was happening again. That knot in her stomach. That pressing need to either prove something to him or prove she didn't care about him—when she shouldn't waste a single thought on him. Not after what he'd done. Or not done, for that matter.

It was like she took one look at this man and she was thirteen. Again. Forever.

"Your mother couldn't make it," Griffin said when she didn't say anything. Emmy was darkly certain *he* didn't feel the need to prove anything to anyone, ever. He never had, not even when he was young and relatively unformed. He'd still been Griffin. "Something about wildflowers."

"Wildflowers," Emmy repeated. Then rolled her eyes, so annoyed with her sister's circus of a wedding that she momentarily forgot who she was talking to. "Yes, of course. Margery wants dried wildflower centerpieces for the tables in the tent at the reception. The bridesmaids and family members are supposed to pick them every day throughout the month of May. And then maybe hold hands and sing around her like a springtime reenactment of the *Nutcracker*. That part was unclear."

"Sounds like Margery," Griffin said. "She always did like the princess routine."

Emmy didn't know why she felt the urge to leap to Margery's defense then, because it was true. Margery had never met a tiara she didn't like, had never encountered a holiday that couldn't be tailored into a vast celebration of All Things Margery, and had been blessed with the sort of lithe, sweet, blonde prettiness that made people adore those things about her instead of attempting to beat her to death with the fairy wings she'd worn more than once and not always on Halloween.

It wasn't a *surprise* that she'd decreed that her wedding to Philip Rollins, the wealthy Chicago financier, should encompass whole weeks and contain so many different events that Emmy had been forced to pack all the separate, ornate invitations in their own expandable file folder. The hayride. The wedding party's horseback ride and barbecue. A spa day. A family-only party. Etc. But that didn't mean that Emmy didn't dread the next three weeks. She did. She'd fumed about it all the way from Atlanta.

Griffin Hyatt was merely the icing on the cake. The six-layer, multi-flavored, monstrosity of a wedding cake that Margery had insisted was the only true representation of hers and Philip's deep and abiding love. That and his bank account, Emmy's more cynical side had insisted.

"I think I'd rather find my own way to Marietta," Emmy said now, because her stomach was still curling in on itself and she was choosing to believe that was nausea, not an unwieldy longing for this man she'd spent the better part of a decade telling herself she wasn't pining for at all. "A half-hour in a car with you is about thirty minutes too long."

Griffin laughed, which made Emmy's pulse rocket through her.

"I see you haven't lost any of your charm down there in Atlanta," he said. "Must be that Southern influence."

Emmy eyed him for a moment that stretched into two. Then longer. And the past was thick between them, turning the air to a kind of fog, and she was still the same girl he'd stripped and then abandoned. Why couldn't she remember that when she was standing in front of him?

"What kind of charm do you think you deserve, Griffin?" she asked quietly. "All these years later?"

He was very still then, as he looked down at her, his mouth something like grim. But he didn't look away. He didn't pretend he didn't know what she meant.

"That's a subject best discussed in private," he said, with more of that brooding jade green gaze of his, making her think of all kinds of things she'd thought she'd banished years ago. Like catching a gaze very much like this one that last summer, across the hot, dry breathlessness of a late Montana afternoon high up in the hills. "Not right here in the middle of an airport. Don't you think?"

Ten years ago, he'd walked away from her when she'd been naked and begging him to stay with her, to touch her, to take her. Ten years ago, she'd offered him her virginity and he'd refused. He'd broken her heart. Emmy didn't want to *discuss* that. She wanted to continue pretending that night had never, ever happened.

Or, barring that, to continue poking at him about it without ever having to address it head on. *Discussing* it might lead to understanding and compassion. She preferred vilification and condemnation, thank you.

"I think I'll pass," she said, very evenly. "And while I'm at it, I'll find myself a real cab."

And she pivoted and started for the exit.

Only to be stopped three steps later by a hand on her shoulder—a hand that kept her from moving in one heartbeat and took the duffel from her in the next. And she didn't want to think about how *close* he was then, how she could smell the soap he'd used in his morning shower and the faintest hint of coffee, how it made her want to sink down into a puddle on the ground and cry the way she had ten years ago.

"Here's the thing, Bug," Griffin said, his mouth in that same flat line and a very different sort of gleam in his green eyes. It made her shiver—which was better than crying. "Your mother asked me to pick your sweet ass up, and that means I'm taking you back to Marietta if I have to tie you down in the back of my truck to do it. So you should probably just go ahead and surrender to the inevitable, because we both know I'm going to win."

Emmy had no doubt at all that he'd not only tie her up in the back of his truck like he'd said he would, but that he'd enjoy it. Worse, that she might, too, if it involved his hands on her again. And she hated the both of them, then, almost as much as she hated this damned *hunger* that only he ever inspired in her.

"Oh, like last time?" she asked in a hard, bright voice. "Because that didn't end so well, did it?"

His hard, beautiful mouth shifted, he stopped walking, and everything went lethal. Shimmering hot, like it was already the height of summer. Like they weren't standing in an airport. Like there was nothing in the world but this.

Him. Them. That same old yearning.

"Are you mad that I got you naked in the first place, Emmy?" Griffin asked in that low, arrogant drawl that snuck in beneath her skin and wrapped itself like smoke around her bones. "Or are you still pissed off that I left you unsatisfied?"

Chapter Two

E MMY'S HEART HAD just about stopped its cartwheeling and clattering by the time Griffin drove the long, dirt road that wound up into her grandmother's land and steered his pickup truck to a stop in front of the wide front steps of Gran Harriet's log and timber home.

God, she'd missed this.

Emmy gazed at the great house that sprawled across the clearing and the mountains that framed it and rose high behind it, the spring day blue and bright all around. She'd missed the arching great sky and crisp air, the mountains and the fields. Aspen trees bursting into riots of yellow over clear streams of icy cold snowmelt. The Rocky Mountains in all their harsh, heart-stopping splendor. *Montana.*

She'd missed the drive into Marietta she remembered so well from all her summers here, with Copper Mountain scraping up into the dizzy blue like it was lording it over the town, high above the other peaks and still draped in a coat of white this early into one of Montana's fickle thaws. She'd missed Marietta itself, from the sweet old river that carved its way along the edge of town and reminded her of a thousand summer afternoons spent swimming and floating and sunning herself to the postcard-perfect Main Street that could have served as the backdrop to one of the advertisements she worked on back home in Atlanta, so quintessentially Western was it.

And she'd missed the winding drive up into the hills, then onto the land her grandmother had bought with her best friend in the 1960s. She knew every curve of the dirt road that wound deep into the trees as if it had long ago been imprinted on her skin. She could smell sunshine and pine through the cracked window of Griffin's truck, and she felt a powerful kick of something like loss, or possibly longing, reverberate through her.

This felt like a hard, deep landing. Like coming home at long last.

And it was *his* fault it had taken almost ten years.

"Still not speaking to me?" Griffin asked from beside her as he turned off the truck's ignition.

Because she hadn't answered his question in the airport. She hadn't trusted herself to speak. She'd attempted to convey her desire to murder him with her eyes alone—and thought she might have been successful when he'd let out a laugh—and then she'd followed him out to his truck, climbed in, and ignored him for the entire drive from Bozeman to Marietta.

Not the mature thing to do, she was well aware. But it

was better than *actually* murdering him, which she was fairly certain would result in jail time.

"I'll let you know when and if I have something to say," Emmy replied now without risking another look at him. "Maybe in another ten years or so."

She could see enough in her peripheral vision. The way he lounged at the wheel, one strong arm draped over the steering wheel, his tattoos climbing in and around the strong muscles of his arm, making her wish she could trace all the patterns herself. She reached out for the door, ready to jump out and flee into the long lost familiarity of her favorite place on earth—but he reached over and put a hand on her arm.

And everything shifted. Then burned white hot.

Emmy froze, horrified. Would he *know*, the way he had ten years ago? Would he *see* the way she reacted to him, written all over her as if in flashing neon?

She stared at the place where his strong, calloused hand wrapped around her bare skin because she'd shoved her shirt and sweater up over her forearm, and didn't understand how he could *do* this. How he could touch her in such an irrelevant, perfectly polite way and her whole body *ignite* like he was gasoline and a lit match and she was nothing but dry kindling.

"I'm sorry," he said, a low rumble.

And it all sort of rolled up inside of her, then. Her sister's unreasonable demands that had left Emmy with no choice but to risk her job to spend the required three weeks here or

sign herself up for an open war with the bride. How angry
she was, though she'd never admit it, that Margery, who had
spent every single summer of their lives complaining about
having to spend *two entire months* in what she called *that
backwater* had turned around two years ago and claimed this
place for *her* wedding. Not that Emmy had any wedding
plans herself, but that didn't matter, did it? She was the one
who had always loved Montana. Surely she should have been
the one who got married here. Not to mention, all of her
unresolved feelings about Griffin and what had happened all
those years ago. It all rolled around and hardened and then
burst.

"I don't know what that's an apology for," she gritted
out, glaring at his hand, wishing she couldn't *feel it* everywhere, in the tightness of her chest and that telltale melting
in her core. "I can think of at least twenty things you *should*
apologize to me for, but this isn't the place for that any more
than the airport was."

"Twenty?" Griffin's voice was as hot as his hand, and
darker. She had to fight back a shudder from way down deep
inside of her. "I was thinking more like two."

Emmy risked looking up at him then, and glared. At that
absurdly beautiful face of his that had ruined her, really,
when she thought about it. *That* had been her first, completely unrequited, deeply scarring, and humiliating
introduction to love. How could anything or anyone else
compare? No wonder, she thought now that she was sitting

next to him again and could see that she hadn't been exaggerating his impact on her years ago, that she'd had entire relationships with less spark and sizzle than Griffin Hyatt's hand on her arm.

"Twenty at the very least," she snapped at him. "And I'm not eighteen any more. If you want to apologize to me, Griffin, you can do it like a man. Over a drink at that goddamned saloon I was never old enough to enjoy properly, or not at all."

His hand tightened slightly on her arm, and she saw his smile in his green eyes a moment before it made those hard lips crook.

"Welcome home, Emmy," he murmured.

"Go to hell, Griffin," she replied, and that felt like old times too, all those summers before she was eighteen when they'd done nothing but trade barbs and hurl words at each other like weapons until they'd made each other laugh. Emmy didn't want to admit how comfortable it was now, like she'd accidentally dropped herself back into the life she should have had, the life she'd walked away from a decade ago when she'd vowed she'd never come back to Montana again.

Something hung there between them, alive and much too sharp, and Griffin's gaze darkened. Emmy found she was holding her breath.

And then she heard the door slam and her sister's trademark squeal, loud enough to scare the birds from the nearby

A GAME OF BRIDES

trees and worse, Griffin's hand from her arm.

"You're already late!" Margery cried from the top of Gran Harriet's stairs, her hands on her tiny little hips and her pretty face already wreathed in a scowl. "What kind of maid of honor is late to her only sister's wedding?"

GRIFFIN WAS GRATEFUL to Margery Mathis for what was undoubtedly the first time in all the years he'd known her.

He watched as Emmy, *his* Emmy, who had followed him around like a puppy for years and there was probably something wrong with him that he missed that phase, shifted in her seat and sighed.

She certainly wasn't a puppy any longer.

Emmy had been skinny as a rail at fifteen, but now had the kind of lithe figure that begged for a man's hands—or *his* hands, anyway. They itched to touch her. Her hair was a silky, shiny brown run through with hints of gold and the way she wore it showed off her elegant bone structure, making him feel greedy and hot. Her mouth was something too close to indecent, and he couldn't seem to keep his gaze off of it. And she still looked at him with those clever dark brown eyes of hers, the way she had as a know-it-all eighteen-year-old almost-college-freshman, like she could see straight through him to the hidden things beneath.

All that, and she looked edible besides, in jeans that licked over her lean curves the way he'd like to do and that cute scarf that wrapped her in a deep blue gauze.

Emmy squared her shoulders, climbed out of the passenger seat, and didn't look back as she walked toward the front steps and her pain-in-the-ass sister. Griffin lied and told himself he was grateful for that, too.

He'd expected to appreciate her. He always had, even before that stupid night he'd gotten much too carried away, which he didn't really think was entirely his fault given *that mouth* and what he'd liked to have done with it, but hadn't. Didn't he deserve retroactive points for not being *as much* of a douchebag as he could have been?

He'd expected that, as ever, he'd enjoy Emmy Mathis's company, even if by some chance she was still mad at him.

But he hadn't expected sheer, near-ungovernable lust to blindside him, pinning him there against the wall of the baggage claim when he'd first seen her saunter into view. He hadn't expected that pounding, driving hunger to slam its way through him, making him wilder with every breath, when he hadn't felt a damn thing for or about anyone since he'd left Jackson Hole last fall. He hadn't expected Emmy's scowl to jack up his temperature like a blast of summer heat and he certainly hadn't expected a simple hand on her arm to feel like her mouth against the hardest part of him, just like all those fantasies he told himself he hadn't had way back when.

He hadn't expected her to push every last one of his buttons without even trying, and maybe he should have. Emmy had always gotten under his skin, even when she'd been nothing to him but the bossy little kid next door every summer. Hence the nickname *Bug*.

But then, he'd always been a dumb fuck where women were concerned, hadn't he? Or Celia would never have left him that last and final time to shack up with his best friend less than forty-eight hours later, which had been the final push Griffin had needed to get the hell out of Jackson Hole—and whatever the hell his relationships had become while he'd been focusing on the business—at long last. It shouldn't really surprise him that even here in Marietta, the place he'd come to get his head on straight and figure out what the hell he was doing with his life, he'd find more proof that he was nothing but a fool where pretty women were concerned.

Or that it would be *this* particular pretty woman, who he'd already made a fool of himself over a long time ago.

The unpleasant recollection of his pathetic history with women was his cue to drive away, duty done and Emmy safely delivered to the family home and the arms of her insane Bridezilla of a sister, but, of course, Griffin didn't do that. He'd never been one for self-preservation. The term for that in the common parlance, he was well aware, was *dumb fuck*. And because he couldn't help himself, he was out of the truck and standing in the drive with another excellent view of Emmy's sweet ass before he knew what hit him.

Before he could get himself in check the way he knew he needed to do.

"It's actually impossible for me to be late to an event that's over three weeks in the future," Emmy was saying in that smartass way of hers, all crisp and a little bit snooty. "Thanks, though, for asking. I'm doing well. My flight was fine despite the tight connection in Minneapolis, not that flying all the way to *Minnesota* was at all out of my way or annoying or anything. Oh, and I'm not being paid for what my horrible boss has decided she'll call 'personal leave,' because it's so much freaking time off. But never fear, I'm happy to dip into my savings for you, Margery. Nothing's too extreme for your special day! Even if it's actually twenty-one days instead of one, like a normal person."

Margery, who had always been pretty in that overly cultivated way that left Griffin cold—maybe because he'd been knee deep in girls exactly like her at Andover and Dartmouth, or maybe because he'd always seen that gleam of calculation in her lovely blue eyes—smiled benevolently down at Emmy like the queen Griffin was pretty sure she already thought she was.

Come to think of it, he'd seen that smile before. It was the one Celia had worn when he'd proposed to her. And then again when he'd pounded on Henry's door to find the two of them inside, half-naked and not at all sorry that he'd finally caught a clue.

Dumb. Fuck.

"Are you done?" Margery asked mildly, reminding Griffin where the hell he was.

"Not really. There's a lot to be said about the brides-maids' dresses. Who looks good in purple? Particularly *that shade* of purple?"

"It's *dahlia*, actually, as I'd think you'd know, given your advertising expertise where I'd assume every little detail counts. And didn't you do that whole big campaign on flowers?"

"I did a campaign on allergy medicine which featured a lot of flowers because they were *allergens,* which feels like a good segue back into the bridesmaid's dresses. Mine makes me look like I'm dying of scurvy."

"Then I'll be certain to make sure you get an extra help-ing of fruit salad at the reception instead of the cake everyone else will be enjoying," Margery said coolly. "Now are you done?"

"For the moment," Emmy said in that dry way of hers that went straight to Griffin's gut—or maybe lower. He was too busy wondering how she'd managed to steal all the air when she wasn't even looking at him and they were standing outside in Big Sky country to tell exactly how many ways she was getting to him.

And then the two Mathis sisters proved that Griffin real-ly didn't know a damned thing about women because they both giggled, and then hugged. Long and hard, like they really meant it. It was baffling. He was baffled.

"You're a pain in the ass," Emmy muttered as they pulled apart, and Margery kept her arm slung across Emmy's shoulders.

"That's why you love me," Margery replied airily, and then her gaze moved from Emmy and landed on Griffin. She inclined her head slightly, still in her regal mode. He supposed that came with the marrying-a-very-rich-dude territory. "Griffin."

"Margery," he replied. "Congratulations."

She smiled. "That almost sounded like you meant it. And here Gran Martha was telling us all about your poor, broken heart just last night. You seem all patched up to me."

"Looks can be deceiving." He tried to look polite. "That Philip sure is a lucky guy."

Margery's smile deepened, and suddenly, she reminded Griffin of a cat.

"Aren't you a good little bag boy," she said, almost merrily. "I'm sure Emmy appreciates having such a rich and famous gentleman as her very own chauffeur. Or is it bellhop? Either way, you can bring her bag inside. I'm sure it's that ratty old duffel, isn't it, Emmy? One of these days I'm burning it in a fire."

"It's a perfectly practical bag," Emmy protested.

"If you're a hulking frat boy," Margery replied. She eyed Griffin. "Though I suppose you fit that bill nicely."

"Frat boy, sure, a long time ago," Griffin said mildly enough. "Hulking? You flatter me."

He resisted the urge to flex his biceps on cue. Barely.

Emmy met his gaze then while Margery smirked at him,

her expression a mixture of unholy glee and resignation—the usual response to a dose of Margery's brand of sugary skewering. But Emmy went straight to his head.

And Griffin suddenly wanted nothing more in the entire world than to take Emmy up on her challenge. To linger over a drink or two or more in a dark corner of Grey's Saloon in town and see if he could get his fill of that decadent mouth of hers. To see if talking was enough, if he could assuage this hungry thing inside of him by subjecting himself to more of the sharp way she spoke to him, so unimpressed with him and all the things he'd accomplished and why did he like that so much? Or if it would require something else, like his mouth licking into hers, which he remembered from ten years ago with a shocking amount of clarity and detail.

Back then, he'd been twenty-one years old and headed into his senior year at Dartmouth. He'd known Emmy had that outsized crush on him and he'd known better than to do anything about it when nothing could possibly come of it.

Yet he'd completely failed to keep his hands off of her.

And in all the years since then, he'd forgotten how tempting she was. How the way she moved, the way she looked at him with her dark eyes all lit up like that, made it impossible to keep his own promises to himself.

But they weren't kids any longer.

This time, there'd be no need to make himself promises for her own good and no need to worry about breaking them. Emmy Mathis was all grown up. She could make her own damned rules. This time, if something started, there'd be absolutely no reason to stop until they were both completely satisfied.

And Griffin found he was grinning like a fool when he grabbed her duffel again and followed Emmy and her sister into the house, like the obedient little bag boy he definitely wasn't.

Chapter Three

WHEN HE SWUNG open the door to his cabin later that day to find Emmy standing there in the gathering twilight looking narrow-eyed and mutinous, Griffin's entire body went into meltdown.

He stared, and hoped she couldn't see the worst of it. He'd been sketching a new design and had been off in that in-between place in his head when the knock on the door had jolted him back to reality. But she was a much bigger, harder jolt.

"Apparently," she said stiffly, "you have an extra bed."

"I do." He still stared at her, like an idiot. Like there was nothing else in his head. Or maybe that was what happened when a woman with a mouth like hers said the word *bed* in front of him; he reverted to age fifteen in an instant. "But Gran Harriet has a house full of them. A much bigger house."

Emmy shifted and let that damned duffel bag slide to her feet with a *thunk* that echoed much too loudly in the peaceful quiet of his cabin. Then she crossed her arms over her chest, which didn't really help things. It became almost impossible to keep his gaze from tracing the curve of her breasts. Almost.

"Funny you should mention that." She smiled, and it was a sharp thing, but Griffin liked the blade of it. "Margery has ten bridesmaids. Ten aside from me, that is. Many of them have husbands. Some have babies. Someone named Colette has a husband, a baby, *and* an au pair. That works out to every spare bedroom in my grandmother's house as well as yours, which no one bothered to count until I wanted to freshen up. By which I mean, escape the endless reminiscences of college life at Sweet Briar."

It occurred to Griffin that he was standing there in the doorway like he was blocking it or barring her way when that was pretty much the last thing he wanted to do. He moved then, reaching out to grab her bag yet again and then jerking his chin to beckon her inside, choosing not to examine the warring factions inside of him—all of them loud and rowdy and a little more hungry than he wanted to admit as she walked past him, close enough that he could smell the apple fragrance of her shampoo.

Her staying here was a terrible idea. Obviously. But he couldn't see any way out of it. The Grans were historically unsympathetic to any deviations from their various decrees. This was their land. These were their houses. Anyone who wanted to come and stay here lived by their rules, or left.

"I don't have a second bedroom," Griffin said as she

walked into the center of the large, open plan space that took up most of the first floor and looked around. Then up toward the open second floor accessible from the open stair on the side wall. "Just a loft with a futon."

He didn't know what she saw when she didn't respond immediately; he saw the clutter of his business and his life. Everywhere. Designs and schematics spread out across the table in what was meant to be a dining area. His desk over in the corner with his big Wacom monitor that he could draw on in the center, his laptop to one side, and the twenty-seven-inch display he used with his desktop and sometimes as a television screen on the perpendicular return. There were clothing samples piled up on the couch and spilling out of a heap of boxes in the living room area and a tangle of sports equipment near the back door.

Emmy turned back to him and he was sure she'd wiped her face clean of whatever expression had been there. He wanted to see what it had been more than was reasonable and wasn't sure why. He had nothing to prove. He was living in this cabin because he wanted to be here. Why was he already defensive?

"A futon in a loft sounds great," she said, and he had to hand it to her, she sounded something like convincing.

"You can take the bedroom," he said, some heretofore slumbering spark of chivalry rearing itself awake.

He could have sworn that that look in her dark eyes then was panic, and that intrigued him more than it should have.

"Oh, no," she said quickly. So quickly he was sure it really was panic and he wanted to know why and what that meant. *Easy, buddy,* he told himself. *This isn't a race.* "I couldn't."

And then they were looking at each other, and it was a little too intense, and Griffin lost his place. It was as if he slipped sideways on an unexpected bit of ice high in the backcountry, and all he could focus on was that needy, demanding thing in him that *wanted.* He could remember her body against his all those years ago in the cool darkness of that barn, when he should have known better and had kissed her back anyway. The way she'd tasted him with all of that untried passion and then melted against him. The heat of her he'd held in his hand that he could almost feel again now, like a brand deep into his palm.

He'd always thought the cabin was roomy. Comfortable. More than spacious enough for him throughout the long winter he'd spent here with nothing but his own dark thoughts. And now he thought the rough-hewn walls were closing in on him and he didn't mind that as much as he should, not when he was looking at her. He kind of liked it.

Emmy was watching him closely, and Griffin was sure that was fire he saw lighting up that gaze of hers then, then turning into a flush across her cheeks. He was sure of it— and equally sure that it would be a terrible idea to do any one of the vivid, starkly sexual things his imagination kept throwing at him, one after the next.

Not yet, he told himself harshly. *Not if she's staying here. Make sure you're on the same page this time.*

Because he wasn't going to make a mistake the way he had with her before. And he wasn't going to make a mistake the way he had with Celia, either. He needed to find a way to be a little less of a dumb fuck this time around.

If that's even possible.

Though when her lips parted slightly, like maybe she was finding the air in the cabin as hard to breathe as he was, what page they were on was the last thing on his mind. He thought, with perfect clarity and that heavy, driving need inside making him feel crazy, that if he didn't reach over and bring that mouth of hers to his and who cared what happened then, he might die of it.

"Want that drink?"

His voice was a machine gun in the stillness of the cabin, loud and harsh. She flinched slightly at the sound of it. Then blinked, as if she was dazed, too.

Griffin didn't really want to think about how much he hoped that was true. That she was as off-balance and wild with this crazy hunger as he was.

He didn't want to think about it. To picture what might happen if she was. What could happen next.

But he did.

"Yes," she said after a moment, her voice thicker than it had been before. He felt it like a victory and that poured through him, electric and very nearly insane. The perfect rush. "I really would."

GREY'S SALOON WAS exactly the way Emmy remembered it and had dreamed it now and again, thank God.

She'd eaten dinner here a thousand times before under the watchful glare of the owners, the taciturn and intimidating Jason Grey and his right hand man, the younger, hotter, and gorgeously aloof Reese Kendrick. Emmy had spent long summers making up stories about both of them in her head like every other girl in Marietta, she was quite sure. They were such *men*. Hard and formidable, not unlike Griffin himself, not that she wanted to think about that too closely.

They weren't a little bit round and very funny, like her ever-exasperated father, still an attorney in Washington, DC. They weren't good-natured and obliging, like her grandfather, who had taken to painting large, still-life canvases in his later years and had taken over the old barn out on the edge of the property as his studio. Jason Grey and Reese Kendrick were the stuff teenage girl fantasies were made of and the scourge of the summer kids who thought their home addresses in far-off sophisticated places made them smarter than the two men who ran this historic saloon in pretty downtown Marietta—because neither one of them tolerated any underage shenanigans.

Or any shenanigans at all, come to that.

All that and Grey's served a mean cheeseburger, if she remembered it right.

Emmy smiled as she stepped into the familiar dimness and found both men right where she'd left them a decade ago when the only naughty thing she'd been permitted to order in this place was the huckleberry pie Margery had always claimed could make a girl fat if she so much as *thought* about eating it. Jason stood scowling in the gloomy shadows at the far end of the bar while Reese served drinks next to a third remarkably attractive bartender with a cheerful Australian accent, as if only stunning men applied for work in this place.

"Are they still so…" she asked as they walked toward the long, gleaming bar and couldn't quite pick the right word in the face of all that obviously unfriendly yet undeniably attractive manhood on the other side, "…growly?"

"Absolutely," Griffin muttered, directing her toward a set of bar stools with a light touch to the small of her back that she shouldn't have felt at all, much less the way she did. Like a bolt of lightning. "It gets worse by the day."

This time, Emmy was going to be able to order something other than a diet Coke, at last. She felt as excited about that as she had about ordering her first legal drink on her actual twenty-first birthday in Atlanta all those years ago.

And then Griffin slid onto the barstool next to her and she allowed as how her excitement was a many splendored thing, indeed.

He'd thrown a hooded sweatshirt on over his t-shirt and he should have looked like an adolescent hooligan. Or something other than the successful owner of a vastly expanding, international business that he was. But he didn't. He did something extraordinarily male with his chin and a particular look, and the Australian bartender slid him a bottle of whiskey and a shot glass. And then when Griffin did something with his eyebrows, a second one.

"You really do ruin everything," she said crossly when he poured out two shots and nudged one toward her. "I've been looking forward to ordering a drink here since I was ten years old."

"Then by all means," he said in that smoky way of his that threatened the integrity of her bones, turning all of them to mush even as she tried to sit up straighter. "Let this be apology number one."

He lifted up his shot glass and Emmy did the same. She felt something darker than mere heat wind through her when he tapped the two together, yet never moved that intent green gaze of his from hers.

She tossed her shot back and let the whiskey roll through her, a mellow fire that wasn't at all helpful when it tangled with all that heat already inside of her. Not helpful, but it made her feel bold. Softer around the edges, especially after a long afternoon spent dunked neck deep in the sea of Margery's college friends.

I just don't understand *you,* one of them had cooed at Emmy, her head cocked to one side so that Emmy had been all but mesmerized by the cunning placement of the barrette that swept her glossy light brown hair back in a kind of wave from her forehead. *You'd be so cute if you let yourself.*

Emmy will never let herself be anything she can't control and call practical, Margery, the raging control freak in the Mathis family by such a large margin it was almost funny, had trilled with no apparent sense of irony.

Everyone had laughed, including Emmy after receiving a warning look from her frazzled mother from across Gran Harriet's large and comfortable living room, and Emmy still didn't know which part of that she found more annoying. That the most controlling woman she'd ever known, who had been like that when they were both under the age of ten, dared say something like that to Emmy in front of all of *her* friends? Or that she was currently sitting much too close to the reason she'd decided recklessness was for idiots like the one she'd been at eighteen, and since then had set about making only decisions that might keep her far safer?

In other words, if she *was* controlling, then that was probably Griffin's fault.

She licked her lips because they burned from the whiskey, and felt the kick of it when Griffin's green eyes followed the motion like he couldn't help himself. She was suddenly afraid she might slide right off the barstool, boneless and lit on fire, which would no doubt count as one of the shenanigans Jason Grey and Reese Kendrick discouraged. It was a measure of how out of control simply being in Griffin's presence again made her that she couldn't find it in herself to care.

"I want to sleep with you," he told her, and for a moment, while her heart pounded so hard it actually hurt, she thought she'd fantasized that. But then he reached over and traced the lips she'd just licked with the calloused pad of his thumb, and she felt a bolt of sensation sear through her, so bright and hot there was no possible way she'd made it up in her head. "Soon."

Emmy thought she might faint. Instead, she reminded herself that he'd said things like that before, and to only sad and painful ends. There was no point getting excited about something he might change his mind about. *Again.* So she shrugged as if men like him said things like that to women like her seven times a night.

"Noted," she replied flippantly.

And Griffin grinned. A real grin, hot and male and *wow.* Like he'd thrown down a challenge and she'd met it, and this was a game they were playing. A game with only one possible conclusion.

It took everything she had not to shiver so hard he'd see it. Or fall off her seat to the floor beneath her into an inelegant heap.

"I last saw you when you were eighteen," he said.

"I remember, thank you."

A little crook of his hard mouth. "We'll get to that night. First, tell me what's happened since. Job. Major life events." His gaze hardened. "Husband?"

Emmy leaned her elbow against the bar, swiveling around on her stool so she could face him. She didn't pretend not to understand what this conversation was about. Not a *getting to know you,* but a removal of obstacles. She told herself she was offended by his arrogance—

But she wasn't. She hadn't been ten years ago. She certainly wasn't now, when anything that might have been glib or reckless in him back then had been so deliciously tempered by the passing of all that time. *And experience,* a little voice whispered.

"I went to Emory and majored in English so I could read books all day," she said, managing to sound calm and cool when she was neither. "I liked Atlanta, so I stayed there afterward. I got a job in an ad agency and have been writing copy for them ever since."

She waited, and so did he, and she would have sworn neither one of them breathed.

"No husband," she said after a moment, and she wasn't sure why it felt like the worst kind of obvious flirting to say that. Or like a green light to a very slippery slope—and she already felt like she was tipping over the edge of it and about to start sliding down. "I broke up with my last boyfriend a few months back. It wasn't very dramatic. He thought we might as well get married. I realized I wanted something else. Like a man who wanted me more than *might as well.*" She slid her glass back toward Griffin and waited while he poured her another shot. "I've heard he's already talking an

October wedding with my replacement."

"You might as well have been a sofa, then. What a thrill."

"That was my thinking." She twisted the shot glass around, watching the amber liquid catch the light. "I'm sure this means I'm a narcissist, but I'd rather not be quite so easily replaced."

He laughed, and she caught her breath at what genuine humor did to that face of his. That beautiful face of his that she worried was imprinted inside of her somehow, making it impossible to really see anyone else. Was that why no one else had ever appealed to her the way he had? Throughout all these years?

Emmy had always told herself he was a childhood addiction that she'd conquered by avoiding him. But she'd been equally sure that if she saw him again, the spell would be broken. Childhood myths and legends were nothing more than favorite stories once you grew up, weren't they?

Tonight she thought that maybe she'd been lying to herself for a very long time.

"I got engaged last June," Griffin told her in that low, sexy rumble of a voice, and she hoped he hadn't seen any of that *imprinting* nonsense on her face. "We'd been together for a few years, she worked in my company; it was all a big, happy team." He tossed back his second shot, then slapped the glass down on the wood in front of him. "Then one day in the middle of September we got in a fight, which wasn't unusual. She said she was moving out. She did that a lot, too. Then two days later she and my best friend Henry—who's also my CFO—took me to dinner. I thought he was there to mediate."

Emmy pulled in a breath. "Oh, no."

"They told me they were thinking they might date someday, since she and I had finally run our course, which was news to me." His smile was fierce and beautiful at once, and something hollow and hot scraped through her, making her wonder how anyone could leave this man. For any reason at all. "But when I dropped by Henry's place later that night, she was there. And they weren't dressed. It's hard not to draw a few conclusions about how long that must have been going on, looking back."

"That all sounds unduly civilized," Emmy said after a moment when he didn't elaborate. "Did you have a polite chat over wine? Compare notes? Are you all *robots?*"

"I left out the part where I punched him in the face and called her a few names I'm not too proud of." Still that hard smile. And it felt even more like a very focused kind of flirting when he reached over and drew a pattern on the back of her hand, the way he'd doodled on every available surface when they were kids. It felt like more than flirting. It felt like history and need, and his green eyes were so warm it made it hard to breathe besides. "I'm trying to make a good impression on you."

"To talk me into sleeping with you."

"God, yes."

"By talking about your ex? Pretty risky move. Amateur, even. Huge potential for that to backfire in a major way."

"There's no way you've forgotten the fact your sister mentioned my supposed broken heart earlier," Griffin drawled. "Even if you've shoved it to the back burner, it's still there. Unless you've undergone a complete personality shift, you don't forget a single thing. I figured I'd approach it head on."

Emmy studied him for a moment, aware that everything felt taut. Pulled tight, stretched thin. And yet too full besides, with a kind of happy glow that he remembered her personality at all.

"I think I'd draw serious conclusions about the length of their relationship and then fire the both of them, for good measure," she said, her tone light. "You're the boss, right? You can do that. I bet that would be even more satisfying than name-calling. Or face-punching."

"Punching him in the face was pretty satisfying. I can't lie."

"I can see that. I think any reasonable person would call that a justifiable face punching, really, given the circumstances."

That hard mouth of his shifted into the small crook that was his usual smile, and Emmy's heart flipped over in her chest. She told herself it was the whiskey.

"I'm considering my options." He studied her face for what felt like a very long time. "I don't care that they're together anymore. I'm sorry to disappoint the Grans and your sister, who all love a good tragedy, but I'm not broken-hearted."

"I'll be sure to pass that on the next time you come up," Emmy assured him. "Which will probably be every five minutes or so, now that all the bridesmaids got a good look at you. I'll have to break all of their hearts and tell them you're *fine*. No need for their tender loving care."

He smirked a little bit. "Just tell them I'm bad news," he advised her. "Or I'd probably care more that the two people who were supposed to mean the most to me betrayed me. And I don't."

Emmy shrugged, a prickling sort of thing sweeping over her, making her feel much too on edge. "Or maybe they revealed their true faces, and what's the point of caring past that?"

She didn't know what made her hold his gaze a little too hard, but she recognized the panicked thing that dripped through her again, the way it had when she'd imagined *sleeping in his bed*. Surrounded by his scent, resting her head where he laid his... She felt reckless and wild, and that terrified her. She knew where that led: her, naked and alone and rejected. *No, thank you.*

It made her feel mean. Or desperate. "Guess where I learned that?"

She didn't know what she expected. But it wasn't the way he laughed then, low and smoky, like the bad news he'd said he was.

"Let's be real, Bug. You've seen my restraint and self-denial, which might have been pretty rough on you ten years ago, but were necessary evils." He studied her for a moment that turned into something smoldering. Something undeniable. Something so stark she thought it was really more like beautiful. "You couldn't handle my true face."

Emmy considered him through the riot inside of her. The alarms that kept ringing and the deep, dark hunger that countered them. The chaos of it all—of wanting this man even more than she had before, as if she'd learned nothing in all these years. As if she'd learned nothing *from him.*

But Margery's wedding was already exhausting and it was still three long weeks away. Filled with too many bridesmaids and the stupid things she'd be forced to pretend she enjoyed, like the wildflowers and her overly critical cousin Beth.

And Emmy wasn't eighteen any more. Or a virgin, for that matter. Griffin couldn't hurt her unless she let him. She didn't have to wonder if this might turn into something it wasn't. She lived far, far away, and besides, she knew better. She knew *him,* no matter what he might have done in the interim.

So she ignored every single one of the rules she'd made up ten years ago, when she'd needed to figure out a way to survive him—and worse, the loss of him and her beloved Montana summers after that night because she'd been foolish enough to kiss her crush. She threw back her second shot and then she smiled at him, and she made no attempt whatsoever to hide the heat in her gaze. Or that driving hunger beneath it.

This was what she wanted. What she'd always wanted.

Griffin's green eyes gleamed. He angled that mouth-watering body of his closer.

And none of this felt like flirting any longer. It was too raw, too real.

"Try me," she dared him.

Chapter Four

E MMY'S WORLD SHRUNK down into that taut, brilliant thing that arced between them, and while she was still dimly aware of the rest of the saloon around them—the music and the laughter and the sound of pool balls clacking against each other in the back—she saw nothing except Griffin and that molten heat that made his green eyes gleam so bright it almost hurt.

Almost.

He reached down and pulled out his wallet, then threw a few bills on the bar, all without moving that gaze of his from hers. Then he nodded toward the door and Emmy had to fight to keep breathing as she slid off of her seat and turned to walk toward it. It should have been easier then because she wasn't looking at him any longer, but it wasn't. She could still *feel* him. The way she always had when they were young. The way she had in the airport earlier.

The way she thought she always would.

Outside, the evening had taken hold, and Griffin didn't say a word as they walked side by side back down the street to his truck. He opened her door for her with a quiet sort of confidence that made her feel lightheaded. Or maybe that was anticipation, so thick and pressing it felt like summers in Atlanta. Emmy slid in and then sat there, staring at the lights along Main Street as she waited for him to come around the front of the truck and climb inside.

"You still have twenty apologies to make," Emmy pointed out when he'd slammed his door and started his engine, to break the silence that grew heavier and more heart-pounding by the second. Griffin slid one of his dark, thrilling looks her way as he aimed the truck toward the hills.

"We can talk about that now if you want," he said. "But I don't think you're going to like it."

"I didn't like it then," she retorted. "When it actually happened. How can talking about it make it worse?"

Griffin shrugged, and it wasn't a gesture of uncertainty. Quite the opposite. This shrug struck her as deeply male and even matter-of-fact.

"You want me to apologize for making a command decision ten years ago. I'm not going to do that. You were a teenager. And a virgin. You deserved better than a literal roll in the hay the night before you headed off to college."

"It wasn't up to you," Emmy retorted, scowling at him. She told herself that annoyance was edging out the hunger beneath, but she knew it wasn't. She was beginning to doubt anything could. "But let's say you were right. Was it entirely necessary to leave me the way you did? Naked and crying?"

"That wasn't my finest hour," he said gruffly, and it wasn't an apology. So Emmy had no idea why it washed over her like it had been, rendering her some potent, dangerous mixture of relieved and even more fascinated by him. "But I think you're underestimating how hard it was to practice all that restraint and self-denial at the ripe old age of twenty-one."

She didn't know what was happening inside of her, but it made her feel deeply vulnerable. Transparent, the way she had when she'd been young and so struck by him that it had felt like a flu. Every time she'd seen him. She didn't care if he saw how much she wanted him, but she didn't want him to see the rest. She was too afraid of what it meant.

"Yeah," she said dryly. Flippant and cool, the way she'd always imagined she'd be around this man if she ever encountered him again. "You looked pretty torn up about it as you sauntered off into the night, never to be heard from again."

She sucked in a harsh breath when Griffin jerked the wheel and brought the truck to the side of the road, coming to a spitting stop on the dirt shoulder. He threw the truck into park and then he simply reached over and hauled her to him. She had the hectic impression of those bright green eyes of his and then his mouth came down on hers, hard and sure.

And Emmy simply *ignited.*

Last time, she'd kissed him when she'd only been kissed

once before, and badly at that. Last time, she'd ended one of their typical sniping matches by simply stepping in close and setting her mouth to his, risking everything.

But remembering *last time* was like peering at the daguerreotypes Gran Harriet collected and displayed throughout her house, because *this* was all color, bright and vivid and coursing through her like a flash flood. *This* was the sheer mastery of the way Griffin held her against his hard body and claimed her mouth. Completely.

Emmy couldn't think. She couldn't do anything but surrender, and she loved every minute of it. She tasted whiskey and that dark, inviting thing she remembered as *Griffin*. She felt one of his hands at the back of her head, holding her where he wanted her as he kissed her again and again. Guiding her as she kissed him back.

Making her burn. Then burn brighter.

Then worry she might explode—

When he pulled back, he was breathing a little heavily just like she was, but he still managed to set her back in her seat with the kind of casual strength that made her feel a bit giddy.

"You should wear your seatbelt," he told her as he pulled the truck back onto the road. "There's no telling what could happen on these old roads. This isn't Atlanta."

Emmy stared straight out through the windshield and saw nothing. Not the stars taking over the sky above them. Not the lights coming on in the houses all over the valley floor and climbing into the hills. Not the wrenching familiarity of sitting in a pickup truck on an old country road she knew as well as she knew her own name. There was too much of that fever in her body and the only thing she could concentrate on was the fact he'd stopped.

Again.

"First of all," she managed to rasp out, surprised she could speak at all, much less in something approximating a calm she didn't feel, "that's incredibly patronizing. You're not my father. He's hiding in DC until next week. Second and more important, is this what you do? You just… stop? No wonder your fiancée—"

"If I were you, Bug," and there was as much danger as dark laughter in his voice then, and she liked both far too much, "I'd refrain from finishing that sentence."

Emmy would never know why she obeyed him then. Or how. She kept staring out at the dark night in front of them, telling herself that it was all *fine*. That her body wasn't in a state of revolt. That nothing had happened because nothing had.

Nothing ever did. At least this time she hadn't stripped naked.

It didn't matter how tender her lips felt. It didn't matter that she could still taste him. It certainly didn't matter that she could feel that kiss lighting up every part of her, even now, after he'd stopped the way he always stopped.

By the time they'd made it back to the cabin tucked

away high on his grandmother's land, Emmy had worked herself into a fairly impressive state. As soon as he parked the damn truck, she promised herself, she would race inside and then do her best to ignore this man and all the temptation he represented, and when she woke up tomorrow she'd pretend none of this had ever happened, which she'd gotten pretty good at over the years—

But when he parked the damn truck, he twisted to look at her, his expression simmering and rueful at once. And she didn't fling herself out of the truck. She didn't storm off. She looked back at him. And waited.

She didn't know why. But she thought it had to do with that aching thing inside of her that felt like magic and was only ever there when she was near him.

"Why didn't you want to sleep in my bed?" he asked quietly. As if mattered, and deeply. "When I offered earlier?"

Griffin's voice was soft in the dark. Outside the cab of his pickup, the spectacular Montana sky was putting on its usual night show, with so many stars it made the night look messy. It was how she felt.

"I didn't want to sleep surrounded by so much... *you*," she said with an honesty she was fairly certain she'd come to regret, and maybe that was why she was whispering. "I didn't think I could take it."

He nodded, like he'd already figured that out on his own. Like it needed no further explanation. Then he reached over and curled his big, warm hand around her neck, rubbing his thumb up and down her nape. She couldn't help the little sigh she let out. Or the delicious thrill that snaked all the way through her, making her feel tight and hot and loose at once.

"I want to do this right this time," Griffin said, soft and intent. "But every time I get my hands on you it goes a little crazy. I don't want you to feel the way you did ten years ago, Emmy. I want to see what we can do with all of this." He didn't have to explain what he meant. Emmy could feel that same insane tension between them, that wild connection that had been there as long as she could remember, as well as he could. "I want it to be fun."

"Can you deliver fun?" She meant to tease him, but it came out too throaty. Too choked, like there was too much serious right there beneath it. "Because so far, that really hasn't been on display. Naked crying and soul-killing rejection, yes. Fun? Not so much."

His hand tightened at the nape of her neck, sending another shiver down her back. His smile was a hard, lazy thing, and it made everything inside of her curl up and shake a little bit, like a warning jolt before an earthquake.

"Don't worry about my delivery. I have that covered." There was no reason that should make her mouth go dry, she thought, but it did. "This is about making sure that this time, we're on the same page."

And Emmy thought that she would rather die than be the one let down easy *again,* which was what she very much feared he was doing. She would, she decided. She would rather die right here and now.

"Oh my god," she said, glaring at him. "Is this about the crush I had on you? I was *eighteen*."

"You were hurt. You just said so. Naked rejection, etcetera."

Maybe she was already dying. She hated that he knew he'd hurt her, that he would use that now, when she'd thought she was making light of it. She hated that it was true. That he had. But more than that, she hated the fact that he clearly still believed that she was such a fragile thing he had to take all this care with her. While *his* feelings were never endangered at all.

Whatever else Griffin Hyatt was, he was so patronizing it hurt.

"Believe me, Griffin, a good cure for hurt feelings is ten years," she said dryly. "And not being eighteen any longer." She pulled back from his hand and studied his gorgeous face in the light he'd left on over the cabin door. "What do you think is happening here? My sister is getting married in three weeks and once that three-ring circus is over I'll be headed straight back home to my life in Atlanta. This? Is nothing but nostalgia and some chemistry."

But he only watched her, his brows slightly raised.

"Chemistry which is sputtering away by the second," Emmy said, more pointedly. "I'm not opposed to exploring this thing, but I gave up being patronized by men who hardly know me about a decade ago. I have three weeks here in Montana and a dirty little fling sounds like an excellent way to avoid my responsibilities as Margery's maid of honor. It would be kind of fun if it was you. But I'd be perfectly happy if it was someone else, too."

And then, finally, with her head held high and a whole lot of nonchalance she didn't feel, Emmy slammed her way out of the truck and headed for the cabin she really didn't want to share with him.

GRIFFIN WATCHED HER go.

He didn't believe her. But he also had no intention of letting her slip off to *someone else,* thank you, especially after she'd used the word *dirty.* And neither one of those things mattered anyway, because she was a grown woman and it wasn't his goddamned business.

His grandmother had sat him down when he was fifteen and full of himself and starry-eyed Emmy had been, in his estimation, no more than an annoying little kid.

You have a responsibility here, Griffin, she'd told him, very solemnly.

It's not my *fault, Gran,* he'd protested. *She's, like,* twelve.

That had been an insult as he'd been so worldly and adult, by his reckoning. Gran Martha hadn't laughed the way Griffin thought he might have if some shithead fifteen-year-old said something like that to him now.

Three years seems like a long time now, she'd said calmly, sitting at the long table in the breakfast room surrounded by glass and mountain views on all sides. *But there may come a time it won't. And you'll remember we talked, Griffin. Because you have a responsibility to that girl, and to yourself, not to go ahead and do something simply because you can.*

Even in his own memory, he'd been sulky. *I don't know what that means.*

You do. Gran Martha had eyed him, her short hair still salt and pepper then instead of the snow it was these days, making her green eyes gleam. *You will. I expect that when the time comes, you'll behave like the young man I admire.*

And so, that night in the barn, he had.

Eventually.

But that was then, he thought, watching Emmy Mathis's perfectly adult body enter his cabin—once again, without looking back, which shouldn't smart the way it did. And this was now.

The glorious now, where everybody was all grown up and no one had responsibilities to anyone but his or her own damn self. Where those three years signified nothing, as Gran Martha had promised. Where there was absolutely no reason for him to think about *responsibilities* when he thought about Emmy.

Hallelujah.

That got him out of the truck and into the cabin, only a step or two behind her.

"Have you finished making up my mind for me?" she asked over her shoulder, and he thought she was the sexiest creature he'd ever seen, with that hint of laughter in her voice and that line of her jaw and that way she moved her hips. "Because nothing's hotter than that."

He wanted to pick her up, spin around, and slam them both back against the door he shut behind him. He wanted to be inside her before he took his next breath. That he didn't succumb to that desire, that he took a deep breath and reminded himself he wasn't an animal, made him feel like he deserved a freaking medal. Or five.

"I apologize," he said, and he meant it. "I'm not trying to be patronizing. I promise."

Emmy turned to face him fully then, and she grinned.

"That's a step in the right direction. Only nineteen more to go."

"Come here."

He heard the way his voice scraped through the cabin. He didn't take his eyes off of her as he watched her pull in a breath, then another, like she was having trouble getting air. He wanted that mouth of hers on his again. He wanted her beneath him. He wanted to see exactly what he'd walked away from ten years ago. God, what he wanted.

And she'd said she was looking for *dirty*. He could do that.

He couldn't wait to do that.

"Why are you giving the orders?" she asked, but her voice was breathy and she was moving toward him anyway.

"Catch-up time is over," he said, but his attention was on

that mouth of hers. "Unless you have any important confessions to make?"

"No." She stopped a scant inch in front of him and he could smell her. Apple shampoo. The peat and fire of whiskey. Emmy. *His.* "I'm all out of confessions."

"That's a good thing, Bug," he said, reaching over and tugging her closer with his hands sunk deep in her hair. "Because I'm no priest."

And this time, when he kissed her, he took the brakes off like they'd never been there in the first place.

It was a high-octane, reckless descent into madness.

It was perfect.

She wrapped herself around him and everything imploded. Just burned away like there was nothing but her. But this.

Through the white-hot haze of desire, Griffin was aware that they fit together with a certain sleek *rightness*, the way he'd tried so hard to pretend he hadn't noticed ten years ago. He kissed her again and again, and she met him each and every time. He felt her delicious breasts press against his chest. He bent her back over his arm and tasted his way along the line of her neck. She made greedy little noises of pure abandon that almost undid him, and he claimed her mouth again, not surprised when he found he'd managed to move them over toward the long kitchen island that separated the kitchen from the rest of the great room. He lifted her up and stepped between her legs, closer. *Closer.*

But when he slid his hands beneath the hem of her shirt, she stopped him.

"Absolutely not," she said, and when he pulled back to look at her and tried to rein himself back in, she was grinning, her brown eyes dancing. "If there's going to be nudity tonight—"

"There is."

Her grin widened. "Then you're going first. I have a very serious personal policy of never stripping all by myself." Her eyebrows arched up. "Childhood trauma."

"Your childhood trauma is one of my fondest memories," he managed to tell her. "Though in my memories, I should be clear, you're definitely not crying."

She put a hand over her heart. "That's almost romantic."

Griffin shrugged out of his hoodie and let it drop, never shifting his attention from Emmy. He reached over and grabbed the back of his t-shirt, then pulled it over his head, and when he cleared the wall of fabric he saw her eyes had gone a little bright and were focused on his tattoos.

He waited.

Eventually, she looked up, and flushed. "You have more tattoos than you used to."

"I do." He felt wicked and powerful at once, and he knew it had everything to do with that look in her eyes. "Want to see them all?"

That delicious heat. It licked through him. It marked him. He thought that if she kept looking at him like that, he'd transform into pure energy right then and there. Like his skin couldn't hold him in.

And then she reached over and ran a finger over the griffin tattoo that covered his heart, and he became nothing at all but fire.

Chapter Five

GRIFFIN HYATT WAS dangerous enough fully clothed. Naked, he was heart stopping. Mythical, like the bright creature he wore on his chest. Like his name. Emmy actually felt her heart stop inside her chest, then burst back to life like some kind of grenade.

"You better stop looking at me like that," he warned her as he kicked his boxer briefs aside and stood there with the supreme confidence of an athletic male, his green eyes glittering and hard. *All of him* was hard.

And his tattoos were glorious.

They swirled and danced across his skin, some of them clearly separate, some interconnected, all of them beautiful. He was a taut male canvas, beautiful in the way dark, forbidden things were beautiful. Seductive and masculine and almost too much to bear.

"I don't think I can stop," she murmured.

"Then this might be a short night." He sounded so lazy, so amused, that Emmy found herself smiling. He still stood there, the bright kitchen lights shining down on him like a spotlight, and looked anything but uncomfortable with it. "And I can't help but notice that you're still wearing all your clothes."

"Imagine if I ran out that door, never to be seen again?" But there was no heat in it, no intent, and she shifted closer to him as she said it.

"We're not kids anymore, Bug," he said in that low growl that moved in her and tied her into knots all up and down her spine and deep into her belly, like that once-hated nickname was an endearment. "I'd catch you before you went too far."

"Maybe that's what I should have done ten years ago," she murmured. She ran her hands over his chest again, then bent to press a kiss against that griffin that guarded his heart. His sigh was a heavy, lustful thing, and it made a molten sort of joy wash through her. "Chased you across the Grans' land, totally naked, then down into Paradise Valley. Hell, all the way to Yellowstone. I wonder what would have happened then."

"Exactly what's about to happen now," he replied, and she could feel the rumble of his voice beneath her hands as she slid off the counter and explored him. The thick planes of his pectoral muscles. That hollow between them. The ridged wonder of his abdomen. "And then you would have left for college the same way I did, and it all would have been that much worse."

She shook her head, and frowned up at him. "You're so

conceited. What's wrong with me that I think that's hot?"

"Not conceited. Just confident. With reason." He grinned. "You'll see."

Emmy turned her attention back to the perfection of his body, because she was afraid he'd see all that naked longing in her gaze. Maybe it would scare him away. She knew it was close to terrifying her. She leaned over and tasted him. Not the griffin this time, but lower. She set a random course across the shapes and swirls that marked his chest, tasting him wherever the urge took her. Salt. Man. The clean scent of his skin, warm to her touch.

And when she got to the proud thrust of the hardest part of him, she didn't think. She took him in her hand and when he blew out a breath, she sank down to her knees and thought she might die if she didn't taste him there, too.

"Stop."

Emmy tilted her head back, but she didn't let go of him, and she could feel how little he wanted her to stop. She could feel the hard need in him, the wild pulse of passion, just as she could feel it moving in her, changing her, making her not at all surprised that he looked different as he gazed down at her. Harsh need had stripped away the laughter from his gorgeous face, leaving something stark and raw in its place.

She felt that, too. God, did she feel it.

"But I want to," she whispered, and he breathed out an invocation to the heavens above.

Then, in the next breath, Griffin leaned forward and pulled her to her feet.

"And if you do, you'll make me a liar," he told her. "In about three seconds."

"If you have to be a liar, that's the kind of liar you'd want to be, I'd think," she teased him, and then let out a little *yelp* when he simply hauled her up into his arms like she weighed about as much as one of his drawings.

The cabin twisted like a kaleidoscope around her for a moment, with only Griffin's green gaze at the center of it to anchor her. It took her a moment to realize he was stalking across the great room and shoving his bedroom door open. And another to register it when he tossed her into the center of his unmade bed—but by the time she really processed that, he was stretched out above her.

"I'd take you up on that, but I don't want to hear about it for another ten years." But he was smiling slightly as he said it.

"Griffin—" she began.

But she forgot whatever it was she was about to say, because Griffin was moving. He slid his hands beneath her shirt and found her breasts with his palms, and all Emmy could do was arch into him helplessly, giving him everything that easily. Anything he wanted, she wanted, too.

Desperately.

He took his time. He kissed her and he teased her, moving from her breasts to her belly and then back again. He unsnapped her jeans and undid the zipper, but made no move to pull them off of her body. He only reached down between them and stroked a finger into the soft heat there, but stopped when she shuddered against him.

"What are you doing?" she asked him when it was clear he was content to stay like this. He was doing something insane with his tongue against the soft skin behind her ear, and she felt it like a desperate heat everywhere else.

"I figure you'll get naked when you're ready," he murmured, making no attempt to hasten her along or hide that current of laughter in his voice. "When you feel like it's safe."

Emmy might have cursed his name. She definitely called him a few. And she was out of her clothes and completely naked and kneeling there in the center of his bed like a wild creature in about four seconds, either way.

"You really are the prettiest thing I've ever seen," he said, his voice like reverence, and Emmy couldn't let that get to her, couldn't let it spill over from all that too-hot emotion she held behind her eyes.

"Less talking," she ordered him as sternly as she could, and he laughed.

Then he reached over and curled a hand around the nape of her neck, hauling her toward him with more of that beautiful strength of his that reduced her to jelly. He pulled her down to the bed and then he put his mouth to hers, and everything turned to lightning.

He kissed her, and she kissed him back, and they rolled over and over each other, and neither one of them was laughing anymore when they pulled apart again. Naked skin to naked skin, everything got very serious. Tense and awed and quiet. Emmy was shaking and she saw something like astonishment in Griffin's hot gaze.

She wanted to say something clever or even mean to break the spell before she lost herself in it—in him—but she couldn't seem to find her voice. Griffin looked faintly unsteady when he reached over to fumble in the drawer of his bedside table, and that moved her in ways she couldn't quite handle.

It didn't feel like sex any longer. It felt sacred.

He sheathed himself and then he rolled them over again, settling her on top of him, and Emmy braced herself above him with her hands flat against his chest.

"Lazy," she whispered, in some rendition of her usual smart-ass self, and he only grinned, though it didn't touch the stark need in his gaze that made her feel so raw. So utterly undone.

"Something like that," he agreed, his hands wrapping around her hips, and then he simply held her where he wanted her as he thrust deep inside of her.

Deep. Hard. Perfect.

Finally.

Emmy shook. She felt the slick perfection of him all the way down to her toes, in the suddenly painfully hard peaks of her breasts, in the rush of *yes* that rolled through her and over her and around her but didn't quite—

He pulled back, did something with his hips and thrust again, and Emmy simply dissolved into a thousand dancing flames, spilling light and need all over him. As if their entire long history was all the foreplay she needed. As if she'd been made to burn that brightly, that intensely, for Griffin alone. Like he'd made her into some kind of comet.

When she could see straight again, she was slumped over him, her mouth to his shoulder, and he was still hard and hot and deep inside of her. That fact alone made her shiver all over again, making that same curling thing inside of her burn anew. He ran a faintly callused hand down her back and made it worse.

"Are you with me?" He sounded much too smug and far too male and she was so far gone she could only smile at that.

"Theoretically," she managed to say, and then everything spun again as he rolled them over until she was on her back and he was braced above her and still so deep inside of her. She pulled her knees up and he sank even deeper, and when she pulled her lower lip between her teeth against the rush of it, he grinned.

And she felt that, too. Like a tattoo across every inch of her skin that he touched.

"You might want to hold on," he told her. "This might get crazy."

"Promises, promises," she managed to say, and he

laughed.

But then he moved.

And everything shifted all over again, then stayed liquid and malleable, as if there was nothing in the world but this magic. This dance. This sweet perfection that made all the fantasies she'd ever had about this man or this act seem like pale pretenders.

This was better. This was perfect.

He set a slow, ruthless, devastating pace. He dropped down and used his mouth, his teeth, his hands. He tore her apart again and again, and only when she shattered another time, only when she sobbed out his name and begged him, did he finally relent—taking her with him when he hurtled them both over the edge of the world and into that sweet oblivion, calling out her name as they fell.

Together.

"ARE YOU ENJOYING your new roommate?" Gran Martha asked.

Her voice was sweet as sugar as she reached across the table in the FlintWorks Brewery, the new microbrewery that had opened in the last month in what had once been Marietta's grand old railway depot, helping herself to Griffin's sweet potato fries.

It was the alarming and uncharacteristic sweetness that put Griffin on high alert.

That and the cascade of images of the very many ways

he'd been enjoying his new roommate in the last ten days or so, as dirty as requested and a whole lot of other ways besides, none of which he even wanted to think about it front of his grandmother.

"I've always liked Emmy," he grunted in a way that did not invite follow-up questions. The people who worked for him would have run for cover at the sound of that tone of voice. It was why he'd started using it.

Of course, this was his grandmother. Martha Wetmore Hyatt did as she pleased—always had and always would. Even her husband, Griffin's long-suffering grandfather, didn't bother to get in her way anymore. And Griffin loved every part of his Gran, no matter the fact she could on occasion drive him straight up a wall. He hoped he'd greet his own advancing years with the same calm certainty and good humor that Gran Martha did. If he only earned half her many wonderful laugh lines and retained a quarter of the intelligence that shone from the green eyes he'd gotten straight from her, he'd be a lucky man, indeed.

But that didn't change the fact that he didn't want to have this conversation with her. Or at all.

"Have you?" she asked now, her clever gaze far too intent on his. "I seem to recall a time when you found Emmy very annoying. You bristled with all your teenaged male outrage whenever she ventured near, which was, if memory serves, often."

"Girls are annoying," he agreed, and grinned when she

arched a brow at him. "In my old age—" and he laughed at her expression—"I've discovered Emmy Mathis is perfectly nice. What do you want me to say besides that, Gran?"

"A great many things I very much doubt you'll say," she said wryly, and he didn't really want to know what she was getting at. He was terribly afraid he knew and no way was he going there. "Though hope springs eternal."

The band below started playing a song Griffin half-recognized, and he took that as a terrific excuse to turn around and look, peering over the side of the long balcony area that offered a view down over the floor below. Flint-Works was one of his favorite places in Marietta, and it had only been open a few weeks. It was a great open space that managed to feel airy and cozy at once. It offered good food and interesting artisanal beers on tap from the towering brewery equipment clearly visible behind the sheets of glass that made up one wall, including Griffin's personal favorite: a smooth ale with a sweet finish called Triple C.

Not to mention, the owner, a transplant to Marietta from the Texas oil business named Jasper Flint, rode a particularly badass motorcycle that Griffin would have been forced to admire even if he'd hated the guy. Which he didn't.

It was a Thursday evening in Marietta in May and that meant the brewery would do a brisk, family-friendly business until closing at 8:30 p.m. in accordance with state laws. It also meant that when Gran Martha had called to tell him that she had a hankering for the burgers at FlintWorks Brewery tonight, he'd had no choice but to bring her here on command, because he was wise enough to know that had been an order, not a request.

And he suspected Gran Martha probably knew perfectly well that Emmy would already be here, participating in one of Margery's annoying and endless bridal activities. She sat at a table down below in a sea of other bridesmaids who all looked—to his admittedly jaundiced eye—like cutout copies of each other. Sleek and manicured and blandly pretty, he supposed, in a rainbow selection of springtime capri pants and tasteful jewelry.

They had nothing on Emmy, who was pretending she hadn't seen him on the balcony and looked edible the way she always did, with that glossy dark hair of hers clipped to the back of her head and that elegant neck of hers on display. She wore a pair of jeans that fit her too well and a t-shirt with an old soda label that stretched across her pretty chest, and that same blue scarf. So smart and too funny and with that ridiculous ass of hers besides. He was a goner.

Not a goner, he contradicted himself at once. *Just enjoying yourself, which you haven't done in a long time.*

But he couldn't stare at her the way he wanted to do, because they were supposed to be keeping what was happening between them secret. They'd both agreed it was the wisest course, because they knew their families and the kind of commotion it would cause if anyone suspected what was going on in Griffin's little cabin.

They'd have us married off by the end of the month, Emmy had said, sitting cross-legged on the kitchen counter while Griffin had fed her pancakes for no other reason than that she'd wanted them and he'd wanted to feed her. *In a double ceremony with Margery, which, I shouldn't have to tell you, would make her implode with rage. She doesn't like to share the spotlight.*

Our secret's safe with me, he'd said. He'd meant that.

So Griffin had no idea why the whole thing pissed him off so much tonight.

"She's a great roommate," he said, smiling blandly enough when he turned back to Gran Martha's too-knowing stare. "Very tidy. Makes more than enough coffee every morning and never leaves the bathroom a mess. A huge improvement over some of the cretins I've lived with over the years."

He'd meant the guys he'd lived with way back in his twenties, but the moment he heard the words exit his mouth he knew exactly how his grandmother would interpret that statement. And cursed himself.

"I'd suggest you marry such an impressive catch," Gran Martha said, much too casually, and Griffin knew what was coming. He'd walked right into it. "But that didn't work out very well with the last woman you lived with, did it?"

"You know perfectly well that I'm not *living with* Emmy." He checked his belligerent tone, reminding himself who he was talking to here. "She's staying with me for a limited amount of time because her sister's friends took every other room in two houses."

That wasn't even a lie.

"Is that how Celia was made to feel in that house of yours in Wyoming? Like a guest? I imagine I might act out in a number of ways if my fiancé made me feel that way."

"Gran."

"One of these days you're going to have to deal with the wreckage of your relationship with that poor girl, Griffin. Or at least hear her out instead of simply moving away from your home in a huff without so much as a single conversation. And then pretending she doesn't exist."

There were so many things that were wrong and that he disliked about what she'd said that he almost couldn't decide which part to respond to. He picked the first one, as it was relatively safer than the rest.

"I can think of a lot of names to call Celia, Gran, but 'that poor girl' isn't on the list."

"She calls me, you know." He did know. It was one more reason to fume. Gran Martha sat back in her seat and eyed Griffin for a moment, like she was trying to read him. He remembered a time when she could do it with ease and he wondered if that resigned expression on her face meant she did, too. "At least once a week."

"You shouldn't answer." He took a slug from his beer and wished he could just get up and walk away from this conversation. But he wouldn't. As Gran Martha knew perfectly well and was only too happy to use against him, he was aware. "I don't."

"And what are you going to do if you win the Great Wedding Giveaway?" Gran Martha asked after a moment. The band below charged into a country song, which was appropriate, he thought. Griffin felt about as close to redneck crazy as he'd ever been. "There's a dinner for the finalists next week."

"I'm not going to win anything." He glared at her. "You shouldn't have signed me up. Which I'm pretty sure I've mentioned one or two thousand times."

He hadn't actually known about it when Gran Martha had entered him and Celia into the town's latest, grandest marketing scheme for her own meddling, Machiavellian reasons. The Graff Hotel was an old Montana jewel, a great monument to a bygone era. It had fallen into disrepair over the past century but had recently been restored to its full glory by one of Marietta's success stories, Troy Sheenan. Jane Weiss, a recent addition to the town and the new head of its Chamber of Commerce, had planned a 100th Anniversary Wedding Giveaway to celebrate and advertise the brand new Graff and all the rest of what Marietta had to offer, mimicking a similar event that had occurred back when the hotel was new. Griffin had been called upon to donate some design work once Jane had learned he was in town. He'd been happy enough to do it.

He'd been less happy when his grandmother had insisted that he attend a Valentine's Day Ball as her date.

Your grandfather loathes this sort of thing.

So do I. With every last bone in my body.

Yes, but you have to do as I say, Griffin, as my obedient grandchild. Your grandfather, I'm sad to say, doesn't. Gran Martha had smiled when he'd sighed in obvious defeat. *There's a good boy. And make sure you look sharp. I can't have a ruffian on my arm.*

And he'd been furious when he'd discovered that Gran Martha had entered him into the freaking contest, with a letter she'd written extolling the virtues of his nonexistent relationship with Celia and Griffin's own life-long connection to Marietta.

"I don't understand why you're so invested in this," he said now, picking his words and his tone carefully. "And don't think I don't know that you had a hand in my being picked as a finalist."

"Are you suggested I colluded with that lovely Jane Weiss in some way?" Gran Martha asked, laughing, though the truth of it was perfectly clear in that glint in her green eyes. "Simply because I happen to be a member of the Chamber of Commerce? I've never been so offended in my life."

She wasn't in the least bit offended, or if she was, she dealt with it by eating more of his fries with perfect equanimity. Griffin ran a hand over his face and wished he could summon the same kind of cool. They'd announced the finalists at a barn dance in April, which he'd only attended because he was a vendor. He hadn't been amused to discover that he'd been named one of them.

"Celia and I aren't getting back together and even if we were, it wouldn't be because of a contest." He shook his head at his grandmother. "If you're so determined to get involved, you should tell her the next time she calls that generally speaking, sleeping with your fiancé's best friend is a surefire way to indicate you want out of the engagement. What's the point of talking about it?"

Gran Martha lifted her gaze to his, then returned to the diminishing pile of fries. "She sounds deeply remorseful."

"Celia is a very practical person, Gran," Griffin said from between his teeth. "It's probably sunk in by now that trading in the owner for the CFO of the company she works in might not have been the best thing for her stock portfolio."

Gran Martha eyed him in a way that made him feel like a very young boy again. A very naughty and disappointing young boy.

"I liked Celia well enough," she said, although as Griffin remembered it, she'd only ever tolerated Celia. Her recent and vocal championing of his ex had come as a highly unwelcome surprise. "But that isn't the point, is it?"

"If I had the slightest idea what the point was, Gran, we wouldn't have to keep having this conversation."

"This is only an observation," she said, and she leaned forward then, her disconcertingly direct gaze boring into him. He didn't like that much, either, but this was his grandmother, so he sat up straight in his chair and took it like a man. "But no matter how many times you tell the story of how and why you left Jackson Hole, there's very little of *you* in it. *They* did this. *She* did that. What did you do?"

It was very, very hard not to snarl at this woman he'd worshipped his whole life. But somehow, he didn't. "I left."

"What I wonder," Gran Martha said quietly, "is when you stopped making your own decisions? When did you become someone things simply *happened* to?"

He told himself it was the insult that sliced into him then, cutting him open like that. Not that her words had any truth to them. Because of course they didn't.

"Excuse me," he gritted out, rising to his feet then, because it was that or lose his cool. "I have to hit the bathroom."

"Because I would hate to see Harriet Mathis's grand-daughter—"

Emmy. She was back to Emmy, and that got to him far more than anything she might say about Celia. Celia was the past. Emmy was... *his*.

"—get caught up in all these things you don't decide. These things that *happen to you,* Griffin. Like weather. Because the last time you involved Emmy in your own little version of a hurricane, she stayed away from Montana for a decade and broke her grandmother's heart. And her heart too, while you were at it." Her gaze was level on his. The accusation was much too calm, much too quiet, and maybe that was why it seemed to tear through him like some terrible storm she'd summoned purely to make her point. "Don't you do it again, Griffin Anthony Hyatt. Don't you dare."

Chapter Six

EMMY HAD ONLY been pretending to listen to whatever Suzie Someone Or Other had been twittering on about to her left for the past fifteen minutes but even if she'd been paying close attention, she saw nothing but Griffin when he came down the stairs from the brewery's second level like a thundercloud.

He didn't glance her way as he disappeared into the crowd in front of the long hall that led toward the bathrooms. He didn't give the slightest indication that a mere handful of hours before, he'd been doing his level best to make sure she couldn't get dressed for the bridesmaids' evening outing. The memory of it still made her shiver.

Because she could still feel the way his mouth had moved on her, the way his hands had gripped her hips while he licked into her, the way he—

"You don't still have a crush on him, do you?" Margery asked from beside her, her tone a little too arch for Emmy's liking. Emmy ignored it, because that was her sworn duty for the next week and a half.

You need to lock all that sassiness away, Gran Harriet had told her after an unfortunate altercation between Emmy and Margery over the latter's desire for personalized gourmet chocolates to grace every place setting.

How lucky for Margery that the owner of Copper Mountain Chocolates is nicer than me, she'd retorted. *Because* obviously *having chocolates made in the shape of her face is insane.*

Which you can talk about at your leisure after the wedding, Gran Harriet had replied serenely without even glancing up from her Kindle, where, she'd announced at dinner only the night before, she kept all her erotica. *But not before, Emmy. Consider it a personal challenge.*

"Of course I don't still have a crush on him," Emmy replied stoutly now.

It was no more than the honest truth. It wasn't a crush if she'd been sleeping with the man for more than a week, was it? Or not sleeping with the man, to be more precise. It was definitely something else. Not that she knew what that *something else* was. Not that there had been much time to ask between all that making up for lost time and experimenting with a lifetime of longing made real at last.

She modified her tone in deference to her grandmother and continued. "I don't know if you've noticed, but I'm not a teenager anymore. I don't spend a whole lot of time screaming into the wind or at Mom and Dad that no one understands my adolescent pain. I don't keep a dramatic journal. I don't have unexplained bouts of hormonal angst for no reason, or a face full of pimples for that matter. And I don't have a crush on Griffin."

It didn't matter what she called this thing with Griffin, of course. She was going home after the wedding, he was staying here, and that was that. If there was a small bubble of something inside her that felt a bit too scraped raw at that thought, oh well. Reality was reality no matter how she felt about it.

"I'm delighted to hear it." Margery settled back in her chair and smiled as she glanced around at all of her too-pretty, too-perfect friends as they chattered with each other and laughed in that particular way some women had, that was all about calling attention to themselves.

Stop, Emmy ordered herself. *Being snide only makes you one of them.*

Margery returned her attention to Emmy eventually, with what felt like a little touch of unnecessary theater. "Because he's engaged, you know."

"Is he?" Emmy feigned a great fascination with the label on the fancy huckleberry soda she was drinking. "Why did I think that was called off?"

"The rumor is that she cheated on him." Margery sniffed. "But he still entered the two of them in that stupid wedding contest, so draw your own conclusions about what *that* means." She didn't wait for Emmy to draw any conclusions one way or another, she simply launched into her grievances concerning Marietta's Great Wedding Giveaway, a topic she returned to roughly fifteen times a day. Even when Gran Harriet was in the room, though Margery knew as well as Emmy did that Gran was on the Marietta Chamber of Commerce along with her usual partner in crime, Griffin's Gran Martha. "Do you really think that I would have had my wedding now if I'd known about this? If it had even *existed* eighteen months ago? I don't understand these people. Some of us plan things in advance. Some of us actually care about our weddings and don't leave them up to the random choices of some backwater town."

"You mean *this* backwater town?" Emmy asked mildly, thunking her soda bottle on the table before her with perhaps a shade too much force. "The very one where you've chosen to have your great three-week wedding extravaganza?"

"You know what I mean," Margery said dismissively. "Who comes up with these things? Why didn't the Grans put a stop to it when they knew perfectly well my wedding was this year? And besides, what couple would think it was a good idea to throw themselves on the mercy of strangers for something as important as their own wedding? God only knows what will happen. It will be like a patchwork quilt of a wedding. Raggedy Ann Gets Married By A Committee Of People She's Never Met."

"Some people like patchwork quilts. And Raggedy Ann, for that matter."

"Some people like Cheez Whiz, too, but that doesn't mean I'm offering it with the canapés."

"Calm down, Bridezilla," Emmy suggested, and maybe

there was more snideness in her tone than she intended, because the look Margery gave her was very narrow indeed. "There are other people getting married this year. Many on the very same day as you. I know it's hard to get your head around this, but you can't actually reserve an entire year all for yourself."

"It's obnoxious," Margery said, and Emmy honestly didn't know if she meant the fact she couldn't reserve the whole year or the Wedding Giveaway itself. "It completely penalizes those of us who actually spent the time planning our weddings for ourselves."

"How does it penalize you, exactly?" And yes, her voice was definitely sharper than necessary. Emmy told herself it had nothing to do with the fact Griffin was competing to get a patchwork wedding all his own, a fact he'd conveniently failed to disclose before they'd slept together one or two hundred times. A fact that, when coupled with what he'd told her about his not-so-ex-fiancée, could conceivably be viewed as a rather gigantic lie. *Nothing at all.* "I think the whole thing is sweet. It's very Wild West. Stagecoaches and top hats. And what they've done to the Graff Hotel is amazing. It's gorgeous. Have you even looked inside? Mom said the renovations cost upwards of ten million dollars, and you can tell."

"If you can't afford to get married, you shouldn't get married," said the pampered society princess who lived in the lap of luxury in a Chicago penthouse and was marrying the very, very wealthy man who funded her demanding lifestyle of daily beauty regimens and ever-changing obsessions with this or that workout craze of the moment. "You shouldn't pretend it's somehow romantic to let other people—total strangers and random vendors—pay for it for you."

"Excuse me," Emmy said, forcing herself to smile when that was the last thing she felt like doing, because Gran Harriet would want that. She stood then, faster than she should have, because that was a better choice than punching Margery the way she'd done once before—memorably—when she'd been a very angry eight-year-old. A better choice, if far less satisfying. "I have to go to the bathroom and vomit. Then weep for your future, Marie Antoinette."

"Right, because I'm the bad guy for speaking a few home truths." Margery rolled her eyes with a complete lack of concern, and then placed her hand on her chest like she was pledging allegiance to herself. "I'm *paying* for *my* cake."

Emmy was ten long strides away from the table before she unclenched her jaw. And she was standing in the line for the women's room with her arms crossed tight over her chest and her hands in fists for what felt like twelve hours before she managed to pull in a deep breath and relax a little bit. But only a little bit.

She admitted to herself that it wasn't Margery's usual display of astounding self-centeredness that was getting to her. That was just Margery, and most of the time, Emmy didn't think her sister even meant the things she said. She liked being controversial almost as much as she liked attention.

Emmy knew what she was *actually* upset about wasn't her sister's opinion about the Great Wedding Giveaway that had nothing to do with her.

She shifted against the wall, smiling politely at the woman behind her in line and then looking past her, back into the crowded main room of the brewery. It looked like a happy, comfortable sort of place where anyone in their right mind would love to while away a few evenings, and there was no reason why that should bother her, too. Atlanta was filled with happy, comfortable places, after all. It was a happy, comfortable city, which was why Emmy had chosen it in the first place.

But almost ten years later, it still doesn't feel like home. Not like this.

That felt like the punch she'd have loved to deliver to her sister, straight into her solar plexus. The wind went out of her. Emmy was glad she was standing with a wall at her back, because she was afraid that if she hadn't been, she'd have toppled over. She shook her head to clear it, but it didn't help.

Air, she decided. She needed air.

She bolted out of the line and followed the hallway until it ended in a propped-open door to the outside. She pushed through it, breathing in deep as the cooler outside temperature hit her. The old railway depot seemed mysterious and grand in the long blue of a late spring night.

Emmy didn't know what made her walk away from the building, out toward the railway tracks and away from Front Avenue, which was still relatively busy this early on a Thursday evening. The Graff Hotel rose up to her left down past the green of the small park that separated it from the old depot, looking much more polished and inviting than she remembered it from her youth. If she followed the train tracks down to the right she'd find the Wolf Den, the seediest bar in Marietta—which was helpfully located across the street from the old Catholic church and the police station, should the sins carried out within by the usually rough customers need addressing on either the spiritual or civic level. But she didn't move. She stood there for a moment, breathing, and then something made her turn back and gaze up into the lit windows of what looked like a sprawling apartment above the brewery and the couple that she could see clearly inside.

They weren't touching. The man was tall and blonde and had the sort of powerfully rugged athleticism that only a dead woman would fail to notice. Emmy definitely wasn't dead. He had his arms crossed over his chest and a small smile on his face as he listened to whatever the small blonde woman was saying to him, as if he found every grand, illustrative gesture she made with her hands a kind of poetry.

It was one of the most intimate things Emmy had ever seen, private and perfect, and she didn't understand why she felt so shaken when she turned away again. She swallowed, hard, then looked around as much to blink back the odd swell of emotion that threatened to spill from her eyes as anything else, and that was when she saw him.

She knew it was Griffin even though he stood in shadows further along the tracks, turned away from her, his gaze somewhere high on Copper Mountain, which thrust up into the sky above the town looking moody and indigo in the evening light. That punch she'd suffered inside FlintWorks still shook through her and she hurt, like she'd sustained a serious bruising from something that hadn't even happened, and she walked toward him anyway.

Because she didn't seem to know how to do anything else. Because he felt like home, too, and that was the most dangerous thing she'd thought yet.

He didn't acknowledge her when she came to a stop at his elbow. He didn't look away from the mountain. She had a brief and vicious fight with herself, but common sense won. Only a crazy psycho would confront a man about his past a mere ten days into whatever their thing was. Because only a crazy psycho, a boiler of bunnies extraordinaire, would fail to recognize that doing so was an expression of pure, unearned jealousy.

And Emmy might have spent some time detailing for Margery how far behind her she'd left her teenage years, but that didn't mean she was unaware that when it came to things like this, it was always, always better to play it cool. It had been true in the seventh grade and it was true now.

So it came as a great surprise when she opened her mouth to make a witty observation about something like the weather and that wasn't what came out at all.

"I hope you and your apparently not-so-ex-fiancée win the Great Wedding Giveaway, Griffin," she heard herself say instead, with a biting sort of mock cheerfulness that would have made her flinch if it hadn't been coming out of her own mouth. "You two lovebirds definitely have my vote."

"Perfect," Griffin bit out into the blue night air surrounding them, shaking his head at the brooding mountain in the distance that didn't give a single shit what was happening to what was supposed to be his quiet, peaceful life. "That's fucking perfect."

Emmy stood next to him, every inch of her practically vibrating with tension, and he'd been standing out here for too long already. He had to go back inside and continue his painful dinner with Gran Martha whether he wanted to or not, because a man did not abandon his grandmother no matter how irritating the conversation. And he should have been deeply alarmed by the fact Emmy had mentioned the wedding contest thing at all, especially in that tone. Where was that siren that always went off inside of him when women got the wrong idea? When it was made clear that intentions had veered off in directions he didn't want to go? Where was his sense of self-preservation?

When did you become someone things simply happened to?
Gran Martha had asked, and he still couldn't answer the
damned question. Because he still didn't know.

But Emmy, by God, was not one of those things. He'd
wanted her for a decade. She was a choice, not a consolation
prize.

"If you want to ask me a question, Bug, you should go
ahead and ask it. I don't do too well with the mind games
and passive aggressive bullshit."

He felt more than saw her bristle beside him.

"I thought I was pretty clear," she said in the same sharp
tone that despite himself, he didn't hate the way he knew he
should, because it was such a novelty to have someone come
at him directly. No tiptoeing around him. No placating him.
Emmy and Gran Martha were the only ones who had in
years. "I'm accusing you of lying to me. Of pretending to
have broken up with your fiancée so I'd sleep with you when
really, you're hoping to win a grand wedding at the Graff
Hotel with her before you ride off into a great big Montana-
flavored happily-ever-after." She shifted so she could glare at
him. "I'm surprised you didn't pick up on that. What with
the pointed sarcasm."

"Gran Martha just spent the better part of the last half
hour eating my fries and ripping into me in her own,
inimitable way," Griffin commented, returning Emmy's
glare without bothering to hold himself back at all. It
occurred to him that there was no one else on earth he was so

completely himself with. That had been true when he'd been sixteen and that self had been seventy-five percent conceited jerk and it was true now. He didn't know how to feel about that, so he kept going. "You think you can follow her act? She's had a couple of decades more practice."

"I think the point I'm trying to make is that I don't mind *following* anyone," Emmy said after a moment of scowling at him. "It's the being involved with cheating when only one of us is aware I'm doing it that I find problematic, you *asshole*."

"Reality check."

He didn't know when he moved or even that he meant to move, but there he was, backing her into the wall of the depot, deeper into the shadows. Far away from any watchful eyes—not that at the moment, he gave a shit who might see them.

"I'm not trying to win anything," he told her when her back was to the wall and she was scowling up at him ferociously, her hands in fists he knew he'd feel if he dared call them what they were. Adorable. He had to fight himself to keep his own hands at his sides, because he was already so used to touching her when he was this close to her that *not touching her* felt like a punishment. When had that happened? "And I don't cheat."

"Are you or are you not a finalist in the wedding contest currently sweeping the town? About which I read two articles in the *Copper Mountain Courier* this very morning?"

He shook his head at her, and he didn't understand a goddamn thing. Not this storm in him that his grandmother had unleashed. Not this growing, gaping thing in his chest that he was beginning to worry was specifically Emmy-shaped. Not his fascination with her mouth, which felt a whole lot more like an addiction. Not any of it.

Griffin only knew he had to touch her, that he *needed* it, so he did. He slid his hands over her jaw and up to cradle her soft cheeks, holding her face still and furious, right where he wanted it.

"Gran Martha signed me and Celia up for the fucking contest," he told her, very quietly, because everything inside of him was loud. Much too loud. Chaotic and wild. Everything but her. "Even though she knows perfectly well we broke up."

Emmy blinked. Griffin felt her breathe, and he thought he loved the way her dark eyes moved over him then. The same way he loved the way she settled into his grip, her hands—unfisted—moving to hold on to him at his waist. Because he didn't have to explain the long and torturous history of his meddling grandmother and her various schemes to Emmy. He didn't have to assure her that yes, it was entirely possible that Gran Martha could do something like this for her own mysterious reasons and who cared how much trouble it caused him?

"What's her endgame?" she asked instead, because she'd known Gran Martha all her life. She already knew what it was like to find herself in the crosshairs of the Grans when they'd decided events should proceed in a certain manner and their troublesome offspring weren't cooperating as they'd like.

It had never really occurred to Griffin how deeply satisfying it could be to not have to explain something that had always been so self-evident in their families. Like reverting to his native language when he'd spent his entire adult life speaking in a new one.

He moved his thumbs gently from her temples to the edge of her lips, then back, and there was no particular reason he should feel that touch inside him as if she was the one soothing him, caressing him.

"I don't know," he said. "She was never a fan of Celia's. It was always the raised eyebrows and the high-pitched, too polite voice when Celia was around, like she was waiting for Celia to steal the silver or run off with the mailman."

"I guess she really is psychic," Emmy teased him. "Just as she's always claimed."

Griffin was amazed that he smiled then, but he did. "Yeah. Lucky me."

He felt Emmy mimic the motion of his thumbs with hers, there at his waist, like little licks of comfort and fire.

"She must want something. Do you know what?"

"She wants me to choose," he said gruffly. "To act, not react."

Emmy studied him for a moment, while the shadows

seemed to cool all around them and the sky turned a deeper blue above. He heard traffic from the street out front and the slam of car doors as Marietta readied itself for a Thursday night in good weather after so many months of snow and ice and gloom.

"Isn't that what you do?" she asked. Her voice was soft. "I mean, that's your job, isn't it? Making money and throwing yourself down remote mountains and whatever else it is you do and claim is fun?"

"Not that you read that article in *Outside* magazine."

"Of course not. I don't find you in the least bit interesting."

Griffin thought her smile then was the prettiest thing he'd ever seen, and far more dangerous than it should have been. It became his whole world. It swelled in him like a single note of music, played long and loud, then echoing on forever. It seemed bluer than the May evening all around them and soared higher than the mountain behind him and letting go of her was the hardest thing he'd ever done. But he did it anyway.

Because they were standing outside in Marietta and it was still light. And this thing between them was supposed to be a secret for a thousand very good reasons neither one of them had needed to spell out, no matter how annoying he thought it was at times like this.

And because he couldn't be in love with Emmy Mathis.

That couldn't be what that stitch-like thing in his side

and that hollowness higher up in his chest was, because that wasn't the least bit reasonable or practical and it was past time he started acting like he was either one of those things again.

Gran Martha was right, no matter how little he'd liked the words she'd chosen or the fact she'd called him out on it in the first place. He'd stormed out of Jackson Hole. He'd refused Celia's calls. He only spoke to Henry about business when it couldn't be avoided any longer, and preferred to use email and voicemail messages when possible. He'd pulled a disappearing act on his entire company and holed up here in Marietta instead, licking his wounds.

It had been a long winter. But it was time he accepted the fact that spring was here. And that he wasn't the man he'd been back in September.

Especially now, looking down at this woman who'd known him before he was *GriffinFlight*. Who knew him in a way no one else could.

"I like the art," he said, and there was no possible way Emmy could know that it was a confession ripped straight out of the deepest, darkest part of him. There was no way that she could see how much this hurt to admit. "I like tattoos. I like incorporating them into places they don't normally go. Clothes and equipment and the rest. I like tattoo culture and, yes, a whole lot of extreme sports. But I hate the business." He let out a sound that wasn't quite a laugh. "I hate *running* the business."

I'm not having fun anymore, he'd said to Celia maybe a year ago, but he'd said it lightly and with a grin, so he could play it off as a joke if she reacted badly.

Had he known she'd react badly? Was that why he'd said it at all—to test the waters?

They'd been sitting in his office talking strategy for another big corporate meeting he hadn't wanted to take. He hadn't been able to remember the last time he'd given a shit what happened in one of these meetings—and the funny thing was, the less he'd cared, the more he'd dominated them. The more he wanted to bail on the whole thing, the more money he made and the less likely it seemed he'd ever escape the behemoth GriffinFlight had become.

Celia had sighed the way she'd done when she'd thought Griffin needed *handling.* That had been what she and Henry had called it, like it had been a big joke the whole company was in on, or like Griffin had been a fractious toddler they had to appease as part of their daily duties. Not that it had seemed like she'd been joking that day.

Grow up, Griffin, Celia had said with a quiet impatience that had looked a little too much like dislike, to his recollection. *You're not a ski bum anymore. You're not selling a couple of t-shirts out of the trunk of your car and hoping for the best. This is work, not fun.*

Emmy's mouth shifted into something wry and Griffin braced himself for more of the same. He was a man, after all. Wasn't he supposed to want nothing more than to conquer the world? And revel in it once he did? Like some latter day Viking on an endless corporate rampage?

"That's funny," she said, and there was a rich note in her voice, warm like laughter. Like there was nothing wrong with him after all. "I don't think I've really thought about it in those terms before, but I'm so tired of the kind of writing I do. I'm tired of coming up with a thousand pithy lines of copy for other people to dismiss and then complain about. I spend most of my time trying to work around my idiot boss, correcting her mistakes and then biting my tongue while she takes credit for it. I'm so much better at managing teams and projects than I am at forcing myself to meet deadlines." She smiled up at him. "We should switch. You be the talent. I'll be the management. It would be fun."

His heart was pounding. He didn't know what to make of her easy acceptance of him, or how much he wished he really could switch places with her and see what kind of fun they'd have, so he reached over and took her hand instead, threading her fingers through his. Letting their palms meet. Studying the delicate bones on the back of her hand and testing them against the pads of his fingers.

He told himself he didn't notice that it felt like some kind of vow, because falling in love with Emmy Mathis had never been part of his plans. He thought maybe, if he ignored it, it would go away. Just like she would when her sister's wedding was over, and much sooner than he wanted to think about.

But then, because it felt sacred where they stood and something in him needed the rawness of total honesty, despite how little it had ever done for him in the past, he kept talking.

"Sometimes I think the dumbest thing I ever did was make it big."

For a moment, he didn't think he'd said that out loud. Only thought it, the way he had on all those nights he'd found himself sleepless and restless and lost in that last year before he'd left Jackson Hole and his company behind. Thought it so long and so hard he'd imagined it must have showed on his face, like another tattoo, but no one had ever seemed to see it. Not in Jackson Hole and not throughout the long, cold winter here. Why should tonight be any different?

But then Emmy's hand moved in his. She leaned forward, bringing his hand to her mouth and pressing a soft kiss in the center of his palm. He felt it like a lightning bolt. He felt it like a blessing. He felt it everywhere.

"Then make something else instead, Griffin," she said, and changed everything. "That's what you do best."

Chapter Seven

AND THEN SUDDENLY it was the week of the wedding, a fact which seemed to bear down on Emmy like a pile of very heavy stones as she sat in nothing but a soft robe in an upscale Bozeman spa on the Wednesday before the Big Day. Most of the other bridesmaids were already submerged in the hot tubs and cooler pools in the private area Margery had booked for their use. The champagne was flowing, there were trays of light snacks and chocolate-covered strawberries, and one by one they were all being led out for their various treatments. Manicures, pedicures, massages, and last minute hair consultations.

It was all very pleasant. Luxurious, even. But if the Spa Day Margery had been talking about forever had finally arrived, that meant Emmy had to face the fact that she only a very little bit of time left in Montana. Only a few days left with Griffin. She found she couldn't bear thinking about it.

Something had changed since that moment she and Griffin had shared outside the old depot the previous week. Neither one of them had discussed it. But it seemed as if every moment was fraught, somehow. Different. As if their gazes caught more, held longer. As if the way they tore each other into pieces whenever they got their hands on each other *mattered more,* somehow.

Or maybe that's just wishful thinking, Emmy told herself sharply. *You told him this was just a fling. And he didn't argue.*

Outside of a few regrettable decisions in college that she didn't think counted, because everyone was an idiot at age nineteen, Emmy hadn't ever really had a fling. It was more than a little galling to realize that she wasn't any good at them. Surely if she was the strong, independent, take-charge sort of woman she thought she ought to be, she could march her way through any number of love affairs and casual flings without a moment's pause. Maybe there was something wrong with her, because she wasn't at all sure she knew how to survive this.

What's wrong with you is very simple, that caustic voice inside of her chimed in then. *It's the same thing that's been wrong with you for more than half your life. It's the reason you stayed away from Montana for the last ten years. It was never an infatuation. You know exactly what it is.*

Emmy did know. Of course she did. But she didn't see any point in admitting it, because what good would come of that? She was still leaving on Monday morning, whether she was in love with Griffin Hyatt or not.

"Are you sulking?" Margery asked, flopping down next to Emmy on the plush white chaise, wearing nothing but an inadequately wrapped towel.

"Is there something in particular that I should be sulking about?" Emmy asked mildly.

Margery's bodyweight made the cushion beneath them into an incline, and Emmy did nothing to stop it when they rolled into each other. She'd been sharing space with Margery her whole life. She might never quite see eye to eye with her flamboyant older sister, but there was a bone-deep comfort and ease in curling up somewhere with her, shoulder pressed to shoulder. It reminded her of long afternoons lying out in the sweet grass on Gran Harriet's land or huddled together under a blanket beneath the exultation of the Milky Way on those late, late summer nights when the August sun finally deigned to set. Emmy adjusted her legs beneath her thick spa robe to spare the rest of the party a Starlet Exiting A Limo experience and smiled at her sister.

"Have you done something horrible I haven't discovered yet? I hear confession is good for the soul. Have at it."

"I've never found that to be true," Margery said, sipping at her champagne. "Case in point, Ella Kay." She tilted her glass in the direction of her girls, pointing Emmy's attention toward a tall, pale redhead with a sugary smile and over-tweezed brows. "She spends one half of her time cheating on that husband of hers and the other half weeping and confessing and dragging the both of them in front of their pastor to talk about her sins in gruesome detail. Whose soul is that good for?"

"Maybe it's time she considered a different, less tolerant spiritual guide," Emmy said dryly. "Or a divorce."

Margery laughed, and it was her real laugh, the one that spilled out like a little bit of sunshine and reminded Emmy exactly why it was so hard to stay mad at her. About anything.

"You'd think that, wouldn't you?" Margery asked in a low voice when her laughter faded. "I think she's acting out because her pastor is young, hot, and single. I think she wants to be his spiritual project. And maybe another kind of project, too, while she's at it."

"What about her husband?"

"Ella Kay always liked the boys who submerged themselves in whatever drama she had going on. Doug is no different. He'll never leave her. She's the most exciting thing that ever happened to him in the midst of his khaki, preppy little life. I wouldn't be surprised if he got off on all her fooling around." She shrugged when Emmy looked at her askance. "Hey, some men do."

"Does Philip?" Emmy asked. She knew she shouldn't have said it. She felt her sister tense next to her, though Margery didn't appear to move a single languid muscle, and she hated herself for ruining a perfectly nice moment. For always having to stick the knife in. Was she that dissatisfied with her own life? But of course, she knew she was. These weeks in Montana hadn't created that dissatisfaction, but they sure had emphasized it. "I didn't mean that."

"Of course you did." Margery sighed. "I hate to break it to you, Em, but I'm actually in love with Philip. And no, not just because he's rich. It's fun to pretend to be a vapid, materialistic little social climber, because that's what people think I am anyway. But you should know better."

"I'm sorry."

"Are you?" Margery's blue eyes were far too calm. Resigned, even, as if this wasn't even hurtful. As if it was no more than what she expected. That made the bottom of Emmy's stomach fall away and her cheeks feel crisp with shame. "I wonder. Don't worry, Em, I don't expect you to be my best friend or a cheerleader for my life. But you're my sister. Try to remember that I asked you to be my maid of honor because I love you, not because it's my goal in life to hurt you."

"Margery." Emmy couldn't remember a time she'd felt smaller or more wretched. "I really am sorry."

Margery smiled as she sat up, and then she leaned over and pressed a big, smacking kiss to Emmy's cheek. "You should be," she said quietly. "You're a little snot. And your pocket is buzzing."

And then she patted her blonde waves, all artfully arranged at the top of her head in a manner that would have taken Emmy all day and every bobby pin ever made, and wandered back over toward the hot tub filled with her friends. While Emmy sat on the chaise, still rolled to the side as if she was sharing it with Margery's ghost, and reflected on what a little snot she'd become, indeed.

This was Margery's wedding. Yes, it was over the top. Yes, it was ostentatious and ridiculous. Yes, Emmy had spent hours every morning tramping around the Grans' land with a handful of her aggrieved and surly cousins looking for wildflowers so her already frazzled mother could make the centerpieces for the tables. Yes, she'd even spent an annoying afternoon with her parents rearranging those same tables that were being set up under the big tent out on Gran Harriet's bluff that offered the best view down into the valley. And yes, those were outrageous things to ask wedding guests to do, even if they were family. But none of this was about her. It was time she stopped acting like it should have been. Like a spoiled little brat who took it upon herself to remind everyone how much fun she wasn't having every five seconds.

Like the teenager she'd been at such pains to claim she wasn't any longer.

She was ashamed of herself, and that was why she dug into her pocket and pulled out her phone, so she could marinate in it and keep her face averted for a few more moments while she digested that uncomfortable truth. But she blinked when she saw her phone's display, because it was filled with a list of texts from her coworkers.

Are you okay? asked one of the art directors on her team.

Are you quitting? queried another. *I thought you were just on a vacation?*

CALL ME THE MINUTE YOU READ THAT INSANE EMAIL,

her closest friend at work and fellow copywriter, Annabel, had texted.

Frowning, and alarmed, Emmy clicked through to her work email account and scrolled through all the messages she'd been more or less ignoring until she got to today's. There was something about an old ad campaign, the usual annoying memos from the office manager passive aggressively cc-ed to the entire company, two requests for charitable contributions to different causes the CEO liked that therefore weren't really "requests" at all, and then, at the top, an email from Emmy's immediate boss, Stephanie.

The power-hungry, two-faced, untrustworthy Stephanie.

Who, Emmy saw when she scanned the email, had taken Emmy's extended absence as an opportunity to "restructure" the team. She had to read it twice to make sure she wasn't missing something, and then it was as if a haze of red descended onto her from the soaring high ceilings of the spa. Red and something else, something that connected hard to that clawed thing in her stomach that had made her snipe at her sister. All that dissatisfaction and fury she'd been swallowing back for years, that she would have outright denied until she'd admitted it to Griffin in the shadows of a microbrewery, because she prided herself on her practicality and practical people didn't walk away from a good job simply because it wasn't perfect.

She didn't text back any of her friends, because there was no point gossiping about this. She'd been gossiping about

Stephanie for at least the last two years and what had it solved? She called Stephanie directly instead, distantly aware that she'd sat up straight on her chaise and was scowling toward the nearest delicate flower arrangement.

"It's Emmy," she said when Stephanie answered her phone in her typically clipped, *I'm-too-busy* way. "I got your email."

There was a pause. Emmy could see the office in her mind's eye. Stephanie's desk in that windowless room that she treated like it was a corner suite in Bank of America Plaza, the tallest building in downtown Atlanta, which it decidedly was not. Emmy's own cubicle outside of it, where she'd been sitting for five years that seemed very long now, in retrospect. She had more experience than anyone else on their team. She'd been expecting a promotion to Creative Director in the next year or so and really, she was aware, should have gotten it already. Stephanie knew that better than anyone, as she'd been the one to institute what she called "monthly chats" but which all the copywriters and art directors referred to as "trips to the principal's office"—and because she was the reason Emmy hadn't been promoted already.

"How can I help you?" Stephanie asked, in that choppy New England accent of hers that set Emmy's teeth on edge. That and the malice behind it that Stephanie no longer bothered to conceal.

"How can you *help* me?" Emmy repeated, fighting to

keep her own voice smooth, so Stephanie couldn't make any of her usual comments about Emmy's attitude. "Stephanie, I'm preparing for my sister's wedding, as you know. I'm two thousand miles away. Yet you've decided this is the perfect time to restructure our team in a way, I can't help but notice, that's a promotion for everyone else and a demotion for me."

"It's my job to make sure the team runs smoothly, Emmy," Stephanie said in her patronizing way. "That's not something you can help with while you're off on one of your month long vacations, is it?"

"This is the first time I've taken off work since I had that flu two winters ago," Emmy pointed out, and it was an uphill battle to keep her voice as calm as possible. "And, as you insisted, I made this personal, unpaid time. It's not a vacation."

"The firm doesn't exist to cater to your demands for personal time," Stephanie said. "Maybe you should spend the rest of your vacation thinking about how to become a better team player."

Make something else instead, she'd told Griffin. *That's what you do.*

It had never been what Emmy did. This was the first job she'd ever had, and sure, she was pretty good at it. But while various coworkers came and went, Emmy had stayed, and the other thing she'd told Griffin was true: she was tired of it. She was tired of writing copy. She was tired of the deadline drama and the never-satisfied clientele. She was tired of

Creative Directors like Stephanie who stole credit for her work and had hated her on sight simply because she'd refused to ingratiate herself the way the others had done, claiming it was *office politics* instead of *kissing ass*.

Emmy hadn't made it big. She'd made practical decisions, one after the next, ever since she'd found herself naked and without Griffin in that barn ten years ago. She'd resolved to keep herself safe after that scarring experience. What kind of person threw away a good job just because she didn't love every moment of it? Emmy had never been that person. She'd told herself repeatedly that she didn't *want* to be that person.

But she'd also never been the kind of person who sunk so deep into a blistering three-week affair that she almost didn't care who caught her doing it. Like last night, when she and Griffin had gotten a little too lost in a stolen kiss in his grandmother's house that had almost resulted in them being walked in on in a very compromising position by Emmy's aunt and uncle. The old Emmy would never have allowed that to happen. The new Emmy had laughed and hidden in a closet like a teenager.

She liked the new Emmy better, she understood then. She liked who she was with Griffin. And she decided right there on a chaise in a Bozeman, Montana spa that it didn't matter what happened between them. Griffin was temporary. She'd find a way to deal with that. But this version of herself—the one who did as she liked because she trusted herself enough to know she could handle the consequences—didn't have to be as temporary as he was.

"I have a better idea," she said into her phone, and she didn't have to fight for that cool, calm tone. It came naturally, at last. "Make me a reasonable offer, Stephanie, and I won't come back at all."

It took less than fifteen minutes. When she ended the call, she had an appointment with Human Resources for her exit interview the following week, a very nice package, and a brand new life to figure out because she'd thrown away the old one.

Maybe it was no surprise she felt dizzy. She sat on the chaise and stared at the phone in her hand and wondered what the hell had just happened.

"That sounded very intense," Margery said, making Emmy jump.

Emmy hadn't heard her come back over. She stared up her sister in a kind of horror, still clutching her phone while panic pounded through her. Had she lost her mind? She had rent to pay! She'd had that job for years! Could she call Stephanie back and get her job again before any of this was made permanent? That was obviously the smart thing to do. What had she been *thinking*?

"Emmy, what's the matter with you?" Margery asked, frowning down at her. "You look pale."

"I have no idea what just happened or why or if I've been taken over by a body snatcher," Emmy said after a moment, and her throat was so dry that her voice was raspy and sounded like someone else's, "but I just quit my job. For absolutely no reason."

Margery gazed down at her for a beat, as if waiting for more. "That's not why you're upset, is it?"

"I can't tell how upsetting it is yet," Emmy gritted out, "because I'm too busy having a full scale panic attack."

Her sister only shook her head, visibly unmoved. "Did you ever even like that job?"

Emmy blinked at her. "I'm good at it!"

"I'm good at being a bitch," Margery said, her mouth moving into one of her cat-like smiles, "but that doesn't mean I should make it my life's work." Her smile deepened as Emmy only stared back at her in disbelief. "And it's time for your massage. Try not to get snippy with the massage therapist, if you don't mind. I can only tip so much."

THE REALTOR WAS a tool.

Griffin had hated him on sight, but that wasn't a good enough reason to punch him. So he refrained, slumped there in the passenger seat of the idiot's Bronco listening to a thousand things he didn't need to know about Marietta's retail market because he had eyes, thank you. He could see the empty storefronts and the FOR SALE signs, although there were far fewer of those today than there had been last fall.

"Stay there," he ordered the other man when they stopped in front of the space he'd gone into the realty office to ask about, a few doors down from the rowdier bar in town. The perfect place to collect the kind of clients he'd want to attract. A little walk on the wild side for the more conservative types and an easy stroll for people like him who hadn't seen their skin without some bold color on it in too many years to count.

He watched the realtor's too-red cheeks get even brighter with a certain fascination, but then forced himself to smile politely, to take the sting out of the order. Because this was Marietta, not the big city, and his grandmother would tear a piece out of his hide if he growled at her friends.

Not that he thought Gran Martha would give this guy the time of day, but he'd lived in Marietta long enough now to understand that small town politics were like tangled roots. He might not see them beneath the pretty trees that graced the parks and would be that deep, lush green all summer long, but they were always there beneath the surface, interconnected and overlapping in a thousand ways an outsider could never hope to understand.

"I'll check it out myself, if that's okay," he said, forcing another smile, and he wasn't surprised when the realtor—why couldn't he remember the guy's name?—dropped a set of keys in his hand and waved him toward the front door, swallowing hard like Griffin was as disreputable as the pair of bikers who stumbled out of the front door of the Wolf Den a few doors down and stood there on the sidewalk, looking ornery.

If he was honest with himself, he thought as he opened the front door of the little shop and stepped through the doorway, he didn't particularly mind what the realtor thought about him.

Inside, he took a deep breath and looked around, soaking it in. It was only a shop, like any other. A glass window in front and a narrow space within. Brick walls and wood floors. But Griffin knew. He stood there with the door shut behind him and that irritating realtor on the other side, and he knew.

He liked the art. He liked tattoos. He'd never wanted to do anything else.

And he had no idea how he'd ever thank Emmy for getting him to finally say that out loud. For making him face that truth he understood, now, he'd been running from for much too long, because facing it would mean a whole host of consequences. For finally allowing him to look beyond GriffinFlight and figure out what might come next.

He hadn't realized how little hope he'd had until she'd showed him how much there was to hope for.

That shook him. He stood there in the middle of what would become his future—he knew it, the way he'd once known GriffinFlight would be big whether he wanted that or not—and realized what he'd known on some level since he'd set eyes on her in that airport: that he didn't want a future without her in it.

She has a whole life back in Atlanta, he told himself then.

She told you this was nothing but a fling. You shouldn't have broken her heart all those years ago, dumbass.

But there was no going back in time. There were only the few days he had left with her and when they were done, he had to let her go. Drive her to the airport himself and smile while she walked back out of his life, because that was what they'd agreed. That was what she'd signed up for. That was what a good man would do, and Griffin might not have as much experience with being a good man as he probably should, but it was high time he started. He owed her at least that much.

He would let Emmy go home. He'd wave her goodbye like he meant it and he'd keep his damned feelings to himself.

No matter how much it was going to kill him to do it.

Chapter Eight

B Y THE TIME Emmy made it home to the cabin—not
that it was her *home,* not that it was even really *his*
home, not that she should let herself think that treacherous
word and all the things it implied about this relationship that
had been over before it started—she was not in a very good
mood. Or she was in a very dangerous one.

Six of one, half dozen of another, Gran Harriet would say.

She slammed her way into the cabin, absurdly let down
when Griffin wasn't sitting there at his desk the way she'd
expected he would be, hunched over his Wacom tablet or a
sheet of paper. She stood there for a moment, unwilling to
investigate the feelings that surged inside of her, as if quitting
her job had unleashed a thousand other things within. The
longing for a kind of domesticity that wasn't and never had
been on the table here chief among them.

*Exactly how many ways are you planning to be a complete
idiot today?*

"You all right?"

Griffin's voice was mild and perfect and too much to

bear, and Emmy took her time turning her head to find him in the doorway to the bedroom, tucking the sort of button down shirt she'd have thought he abhorred into a pair of trousers much nicer than his usual jeans. She could smell his soap from across the room. She could see the dampness in his black hair.

And there was no reason at all she should feel like crying.

She told herself it was this tornado inside of her instead. It was tearing everything up and flinging what it didn't destroy back down and she had no idea how to go about putting herself back together.

"My sister pointed out to me that I've been acting like a little brat for the past two weeks," she said. Possibly with more aggression than necessary, she thought, when Griffin's green eyes narrowed.

But his voice was as calm as it had been before. "Surely that particular pot is way blacker than any kettle could ever be."

"Only if you think it's reasonable for a maid of honor to storm around muttering and rolling her eyes and generally being a big old raincloud over the proceedings," she retorted, which was, she was still ashamed to admit, a fairly adequate description of her behavior in and around the wedding festivities since she'd arrived in Montana. "When she's not running off to have sex with the next door neighbor, that is."

He eyed her for a moment. "Why do I feel like there's no way for me to participate in this conversation without it becoming my fault?"

"It's already your fault." She hadn't moved from her position in front of the door and she curled her toes into the floor beneath her, not caring if he could see her do it because of the pedicure-friendly flip-flops she was wearing, because she couldn't let herself drift over to him the way she wanted. He was worse than alcohol, all blackouts and bad behavior and regret. And she craved him far more than she'd ever wanted a drink. "I quit my job."

His smile was like light and Emmy didn't want light. She wanted darkness and brooding. She wanted this raging *thing* in her to cause damage, to the two of them most of all. Maybe then she'd find a way to make sense of it.

"Good for you," he said.

"How is that good for me?" She took a step toward him and stopped herself, cursing at her own weakness. At the magnetic compulsion that made it impossible to keep her distance from him. How was she going to leave him on Monday? "I'm not rich. I'm not the widely celebrated creator of a lifestyle brand that everyone wants a piece of. I write stupid commercials about fucking allergies and I don't even enjoy it anymore. But it's the life I built. It's safe and it's solid and it's careful and peaceful and *mine*. And I threw a hand grenade in the middle of it for absolutely no reason except a single conversation with you."

It was only when she stopped that she realized she'd been yelling. Her last boyfriend had hated it when she did that.

He'd pulled himself up into the very picture of offended dignity and had walked away from her, saying things like, *why don't you tell me when we can discuss this like adults, Emmy. Your volume is inappropriate.*

But Griffin's green eyes gleamed. He propped a shoulder against the doorjamb, crossed his arms over his chest, and laughed at her. Like all the yelling in the world wouldn't bother him at all, and wasn't there something wrong with her that she found that so attractive?

"I didn't tell you to go kamikaze on your job, Bug. That was all you. I hope you asked for a decent severance package."

"Yes," she said, and her voice sounded far away then, even to her own ears, because the tornado was spinning too fast and ripping her apart, and maybe she should have been a little more careful what she'd wished for, because this *hurt*. "As a matter of fact, I did. And my boss was only too happy to give it to me, because she hates my guts and was thrilled to get me out of there."

"Sounds like you should be thanking me, then," he pointed out, still leaning there, looking powerful and beautiful and not in the least bit intimidated by her volume or her anger. Her attitude. If anything, that heat in his green gaze made her think he liked it. "I can think of a few ways you can go about that."

Emmy sniffed. It was such an excellent rendition of Margery's patented sniff of pure, snooty dismissal that

Griffin's brows arched up, and Emmy couldn't help but smile herself. Which completely ruined the temper tantrum she was trying to have.

The tornado raged on inside of her, but she found that the longer she looked at him, the more she could ignore it. The more it felt like only a little storm after all, a dance of thunder and a shake of rain, and no need for all the theatrics.

"I'm a lady," she said primly, which made them both grin. "Why don't you take me out to dinner first, for a change? Put a little work into it."

He straightened then. "I'd like to do that. But I can't." He shook his head. "There's a dinner for the wedding contest finalists tonight. I'd blow it off, but Gran Martha might take that as a challenge and nobody wants that. So I'm going to go and corner the woman running this whole thing and stop this at the source."

And a kind of hush fell between them. Emmy didn't know what it meant. She was covered in massage lotion, wearing nothing but yoga pants and a sweatshirt with her hair scraped back into a messy knot, and yet when his gaze moved over her she felt beautiful. Elegant beyond measure. Warm and flushed and entirely his. Like nothing existed in all the world but the two of them, or ever would.

It would only be a few more days, she reminded herself, dazed. So what was the point of pretending? Of testing her resolve when she had none? She wanted to spend every last second of it with him. She wanted to hoard every single memory of him, of this, that she could cram into her brain and imprint on her body. And she'd worry about whether or not she should feel shame for that later.

"Is there a reason you're not inviting me?" she asked. She dropped her bag on the floor beside her and started toward him, watching the fire flicker in his gaze, feeling her body ready itself for him that easily. By the time she made it across the great room to stand in front of him, her nipples were tight and she could feel the heat between her legs. "Because the more time I spend on my own, Griffin, the less inventively thankful I'm likely to feel."

He laughed as hauled her up against him, tipping her breasts into his chest and running his hands down her back to cup her bottom. It was so easy now. So slick and perfect, the way they came together. Like they'd been doing this for years, not weeks.

"I would," he said, "but they're going to think you're Celia. And I'm pretty sure that's a great way to make certain you never touch me again. Which is not in the plan."

Emmy wrapped her arms around his neck and then surged up toward him. He lifted her or she jumped or maybe it was both, and then he was holding her there against him as she wrapped her legs around his hips. He took her mouth, hard, and she dug her hands into all that marvelous raw silk that was his hair, and when they came up for air he was bearing her down into the bed and settling himself on top of her.

And it was perfect. It was always so devastatingly perfect.

Maybe it was the fire that only burned brighter the more time she spent with him. Maybe she really had lost her mind today. Maybe the only way through the next few days was to simply burn as bright as possible before the inevitable dark that would follow. Emmy didn't know.

"I can be Celia for a few hours," she said. It wouldn't kill her. She didn't think.

Griffin looked startled. Then he let out a bark of laughter.

"No, you really can't. Thank God."

"Obviously I meant that I can *play* her for one night while you try to extricate yourself from a Gran Scheme," Emmy said loftily. "Or allow people to think I'm her, whatever. How hard can it be? From what you've said, all it takes is being kind of mean to you and then leaving."

Griffin eyed her like he couldn't decide whether to take offense at that or laugh, and Emmy probably should have cared about that more than she did. But instead she courted the edge of it, the sharpness. Like she was digging her fingers deep into a nearly healed scrape. It hurt as much as it felt good.

"Watch yourself, Bug," he said, but she could feel him, hard and heavy between her legs, pressing into her. "You have a tendency to let your mouth write checks your body can't cash. You're lucky I think that's cute."

And she knew he felt what she did. The immensity and

the fear. The fire and the knot in her chest when she drew breath that she suspected meant all kinds of things she'd have nothing but time to brood about later.

Next week, when this was over and she was back in Atlanta and jobless. Next week, when she'd be alone again in what remained of the safety and security she'd spent all these years building in reaction to exactly this ten years ago. None of which was the least bit appealing to her at the moment. Looking up into those green eyes of his, Emmy could hardly remember who she'd been before he'd picked her up in the airport. She didn't want to remember.

"If I wanted a lecture on financial security I'd talk to my soon-to-be brother-in-law," she told him, moving her hips against his and laughing when he groaned. "As he's the King of Money and most of Chicago besides."

"Fine," he said, his hands moving to take their own kind of vengeance against her slippery, lotioned skin, in the best possible way. "If you insist, you can pretend to be my ex-girlfriend."

"Ex-*fiancée*," she corrected him with what little breath she had left.

"Whatever," Griffin muttered, and then he grinned up at her as his hands got more serious. "You realize that it might be hard to keep this a secret if you're parading around pretending to be mine."

She liked the way he said that. *Mine.* She wished she was. Oh, how she wished she was.

"Don't be silly," she said, though her voice was a little too rough and she could see all the things she felt, the tornado inside her and the words she wouldn't say out loud, reflected in his green gaze. "I'm just helping you. What are friends for?"

"Yeah," he said, dropping his mouth to her neck, with a rumble in his voice that made her shiver. "Friends are exactly what we are."

And then he made them very late for dinner.

THE FINALISTS' DINNER was a cheerful affair in the Italian restaurant in town, filled with representatives from the Graff Hotel, a reporter from the local paper, and all the members of the Chamber of Commerce who had helped bring the Great Wedding Contest into being. Griffin didn't introduce Emmy as *Celia,* he simply let the people he greeted draw their own conclusions, and Emmy thought she was perfectly fine with that until she sat down at a table and found herself flanked by the last two people she wanted to see tonight.

The Grans.

Who she adored, but who would see far more than she wanted them to see. Emmy steeled herself.

"Lovely party," Gran Harriet murmured from the left. She was dressed as she always was, in a selection of scarves that brought out the sparkle in her eyes and her good pair of boots, her long white hair arranged in one of the complicated buns she favored that Emmy had always thought made her look like a rodeo queen.

"It surely is," Gran Martha agreed. She wore her white hair short, preferred chunky jewelry to scarves, and kept her hands folded in her lap as if she weren't evil, her green gaze on the crowd and a smile on her lips. "There isn't much better than celebrating true love, is there?"

"Everyone loves a wedding," Gran Harriet agreed.

"Hi guys," Emmy said brightly. Foolishly. "Great party, isn't it? Did you see all those pastries waiting on the dessert table? That new bakery in town is pretty amazing."

Gran Harriet shook her head as if that pained her, while on her other side, Gran Martha sighed, and Emmy supposed she couldn't blame them. She felt about the same. She scanned the crowd for Griffin, but he was nowhere to be seen. There were all the other happy couples, holding hands and glowing and looking adorable, and Emmy told herself that had nothing to do with how tight her jaw felt.

"A dinner party for engaged couples competing for an all-expense paid wedding here in Marietta seems like a strange first date," Gran Harriet observed after a moment.

"I'm not on a date. Griffin and I aren't *dating*."

But Emmy's voice squeaked the way it had when her grandmother had—literally—caught her with both her hands deep in the cookie jar back when she was a kid, and she felt herself flush as both women smiled.

"That would be ridiculous," she gritted out, wishing her cheeks didn't feel like a red-hot grill the Grans could toast their smug little smiles on. "We're friends. Griffin has been nice enough to let me stay in the cabin with him, that's all."

"That's my grandson," Gran Martha murmured, her tone dry. "He's renowned the world over for being *nice.* A credit to the family."

"This is like a nightmare," Griffin said from the other side of the table. His gaze was dark, though amusement glittered there, and he shook his head as he regarded the three of them. "Come here, Emmy. Quickly. You can ignore Scylla and Charybdis. They're all bark and no bite."

"Then I've been doing it all wrong all these years," his grandmother said.

"You really need to sharpen your teeth, Martha," Gran Harriet murmured. "What's the point of being a matriarch if you can't rule with fear?"

Emmy shot to her feet and rounded the table and came up maybe a little too hard against Griffin's side. She was keenly aware that both of the Grans watched his arm come around her with an ease that *said things,* then the way she balanced herself with a far too familiar hand on his abdomen, and for a moment they were all frozen in place, smiling blandly at each other.

"Remind me, Harriet," Gran Martha said after a moment, her green gaze a lot like her grandson's as she directed it straight at him. "When we were roommates, lo these many decades ago, did we attend dinner parties with our arms wrapped tightly around each other?"

"We did not."

Emmy tried to ease back from Griffin but he only tightened his grip, and she let him. She told herself it was that or struggle right there in front of the entire Chamber of Commerce and half of Marietta, but she knew better. She'd do anything to touch him, even here. Even while being called out for it.

And Gran Martha was still talking, still smiling in that too-knowing way of hers. "Did we snuggle up against each other in public places?"

"Only if it was cold, I'd imagine. Remember? Those Boston winters were murder."

Gran Martha nodded sagely. "And to your recollection, was there ever a time that we pretended to be a romantic couple, for any reason?"

"Certainly not." Gran Harriet's smile was worse, Emmy thought, because it was directed straight at her. "Those were different times, of course. But friendship is friendship. Roommates are roommates. And this—"

"Is none of your business," Griffin said firmly. "This conversation is over."

"Whatever you say, dear," Gran Martha replied.

"Darling boy," Gran Harriet cooed.

Like the sweet old things they most assuredly were not.

Griffin steered Emmy away from the table, back into the crowd, and she couldn't seem to do anything but shake her head at him. "You realize you just made that worse, don't you?"

He laughed. "You say that like there was any possibility it wasn't always going to go down exactly like that. You know better."

"This is terrible."

"It is."

Emmy felt faint.

"My entire extended family and a good portion of yours are descending on Marietta as we speak. We have the Grans' family dinner tomorrow night and the rehearsal dinner the next and the whole wedding on Saturday and Griffin, you might as well have stood up and made an announcement at each and every one of those occasions that we're sleeping together."

"Breathe, Bug." He smiled down at her, and the room fell away, as it always did. He was so beautiful it made her eyes sting, or that's what she told herself was the reason. It wasn't that she'd stopped hating that nickname and come to love it instead, despite herself. It wasn't that tender look in his green eyes that she wanted so badly to believe *meant things*. Of course not. "Would it really be the end of the world if this wasn't a secret?"

GRIFFIN DISCOVERED HE was holding his breath while Emmy considered her answer.

He shouldn't have asked, he knew. But he was already having trouble letting her go. He hadn't liked that she'd been out of his sight while he'd tried to nail down the wedding contest's organizer, the always-on-the-move Jane Weiss. He'd tracked the woman back and forth across the restaurant, one eye on Jane's black bob as she moved in and out of various groups and was always too busy to talk to him, and the other searching for Emmy like he was afraid she'd already bolted.

It felt too much like the real thing, coming at him like a train, that no amount of loaded questions could change.

"No," she said softly, her dark eyes luminous as they met his, and something so much like shy it made his heart somersault inside his chest. "It wouldn't be the end of the world."

He didn't know he was moving, but he took both her hands in his and he thought it was possible he could spend the rest of his life just like this. Her hair was down for once, tumbling to her shoulders and glossy in the overhead lights. She was wearing a cute little wrap dress that flirted with her lean curves and made him want nothing more than to unwrap it and reveal her. Then taste every inch of her like this fire between them was new.

You're still such a dumb fuck, he told himself. *You can't even do this right.*

"Emmy," he said then, because he couldn't help himself and he wasn't certain he'd want to if he could. "I have to ask you something."

It was an echo of that night long ago and he saw that she

remembered it when she smiled, their history a bright, hot ghost between them right there in the middle of a crowded party, their grandmothers no doubt watching their every move. Griffin didn't care.

Do you still have that crush on me? he'd asked ten years ago, so full of himself and so arrogant, because he'd already known the answer. It had never been in any doubt, not in years. He'd seen it all over her face every time she'd looked at him since she'd turned thirteen.

No, she'd lied. They'd both known she was lying. She'd blushed and he'd grinned. *Who would have a crush on you? You're awful.*

He'd been close to her then. He'd propped an arm up over her head and leaned into her, his mouth so close to hers he'd been able to feel it when her breath had come in short little pants. And he hadn't cared what he'd been *supposed* to do just then. He'd wanted a taste of her. He still did.

Too bad, he'd said, because he really had been awful. *I thought you might want to kiss me. But only if you still had a crush on me, of course.*

Back then, she'd called him arrogant and he'd smirked, they'd moved closer, and then she'd kissed him after all. He couldn't imagine, now, how he'd managed to walk away.

"No," Emmy whispered now, still looking up at him in that way that made his chest feel tight. "I don't have a crush on you, Griffin. That would be a whole lot easier."

Her meaning flowed through him, the electricity of it

arcing between them, setting him on fire, making him feel something like giddy and drunk and wild all at once. His hands tightened around hers. He had to remind himself where they were, and even then, he wasn't sure he cared.

"Emmy—" he started, but she was smiling up at him and he didn't know what he wanted to say, only that she felt this, too. *She felt this.*

What else could possibly matter?

"Griffin?"

It took him a long, hard minute to place the voice. To understand that Emmy wasn't the one who had said his name and that worse than that, he recognized who had. But it didn't make any sense.

He turned slightly, still holding Emmy's hands, not really sure he was breathing properly, and so his first thought was that he was hallucinating. That all the things roaring and pounding and surging their way through him were making him lose his mind entirely.

Because there was no way she could be walking toward him, cutting through the crowd, her eyes on him the way they were. There was absolutely no way this could be happening, especially not right now.

Not right now.

She was wearing more clothes than the last time he'd seen her, and he'd forgotten that she really was pretty, in that easy, athletic way he'd always liked. Her shoulders were a little broad because she was strong and she still walked like she'd rather be running, her toffee-colored hair smoothed back into a slick ponytail and that hopeful smile on her mouth, and she was the last person on Earth Griffin wanted to see.

He felt Emmy tug her hands away and he felt nothing but empty, then, but he stood there like he'd turned to stone and waited until this particular apparition stopped in front of him.

Not now, he thought again, but nothing happened. She was still right there.

Her eyes flicked to Emmy and then back to him and her smile didn't dim, precisely, but she didn't look back at Emmy, either.

"It's been a long time," she said quietly.

"Not long enough."

He hadn't meant to say that and especially not the way he did, because it sounded like he cared when he didn't. The thing he truly cared about made a soft little sound beside him, like she'd been kicked in the stomach, and he hated it. He hated all of this.

"Celia," he said, and he noticed she was still wearing the ring he'd put on her finger, a detail that made him want to tear the whole place down because what could she possibly be thinking. "What the hell are you doing here?"

"What does it look like?" she replied, and she tilted her chin up like she was ready to go a few rounds, whether he wanted to or not. "You should have answered my calls. I'm here to win us a wedding."

Chapter Nine

CELIA WAS STAYING in the Graff Hotel, in one of the newly renovated suites that fairly burst with Old West ambiance and Victorian elegance. Griffin probably would have liked it a lot more if he wasn't so furious.

He stood by the windows that looked down Front Avenue, toward FlintWorks Brewery at the old railway depot where Emmy had changed everything for him and past it, to the little shop he'd put an offer on before he'd left the realtor's office this afternoon. This was his future. This was what he wanted.

But his past was standing behind him in a tight black dress and he supposed he'd been avoiding her long enough.

"Where's Henry?" he asked.

He could see Celia in the reflection of the window, standing to one side of the couch in her sitting area, her hands wrapped around her middle. He knew what that meant. He knew she was hurting. And while that didn't matter to him the way it might have once, he found he couldn't pretend he didn't care, either.

MEGAN CRANE

"Who was that woman you were with?" she asked.

He laughed as he turned to face her, though it wasn't a good sound. "Really?"

"You looked happy, that's all." Celia had the grace to look uncomfortable. "That's what I meant. I can't remember the last time I thought you looked happy."

"It doesn't matter who she is," he said instead of addressing that, and all the reasons he hadn't been able to tell her how unhappy he'd been. "You scared her off. Was that the goal?"

Emmy had excused herself, smiled at Celia as if delighted to meet her, and then fled. And the only thing he wanted to do was chase after her, but he couldn't. Not until he put his past behind him, at last. How could he move on until he did?

Was that what Gran Martha had been trying to tell him?

"Did my grandmother set this up?" he asked, because this seemed unduly cruel for the Grans. They liked to push and poke, but they rarely threw their relatives off of the kind of cliff this had been tonight. And he couldn't imagine they'd want to hurt Emmy, much less let him do it.

"No." Celia shook her head to emphasize that. "She told me to write you a letter if I wanted to talk to you. But I did a little looking online and I saw that you and I were entered in this wedding contest and I... hoped."

Griffin only looked at her. And for the first time in a long while, he let himself remember. It hadn't all been

128

handling and deceit. He'd loved her as much as he could have loved anyone back then, when he'd thought he had no choice but to storm his way up the corporate ladder. That version of him had meant to marry Celia. They'd talked about kids and a long future together, and he'd wanted that. He was sure he must have wanted that. But he couldn't see any of it any longer. It was like looking at someone else's photographs of a time he hardly remembered anymore, and that wasn't just Emmy's influence. It was all these long months away from a life he should have mourned and missed, but hadn't.

"I should have taken your calls," he said now. "I shouldn't have let this all drag out."

"You were pissed." She shrugged, and her mouth did that thing it did when she was trying not to cry. "You had a right to be pissed."

"You and Henry didn't…?"

He had no idea where he wanted to go with that question and was glad when she blew out a breath and answered it anyway.

"It didn't last long." She held herself tighter, but she didn't look away. "I don't think he can forgive himself for what he did to you." Her smile then was tinged with something bitter. "I've always liked that about both of you, you know. You're good, decent people. I'm really not."

He would have agreed earlier today, but that was his pride talking. Everything seemed a lot more complicated now. A lot more shaded with grey. He thought of all the questions he'd wanted to ask her at different points, when he'd sat there in the cabin and indulged his temper—how long she'd been with Henry, if she'd cheated on him before, if she had, how many times—and none of them seemed worth asking any longer. What did any of that matter now? He'd moved on a long time ago. Maybe before he'd left Jackson Hole.

She'd done him a favor.

"You're going to meet the right person, Celia," he said then, and he meant it. "And it's going to be easy. Not like us. Not all the back and forth, the fighting. It's going to make sense."

"It wasn't all bad," she whispered. "Not all of it."

"No," he agreed after a moment. "Not all of it. But if it's that hard to do the right thing, it's probably because it's not the right thing at all."

She nodded once, jerkily, and she took in a sharp breath, and when she looked back at him any trace of emotion in her gaze was gone. He didn't tell her that he'd always admired that she could do that, that she could hide anything, because he thought she'd take it as a dig. She stripped the ring he'd given her off her finger and held it out to him.

"This is yours."

"I actually Googled that. You're only supposed to give it back if it's an heirloom. It's not, so it's yours."

"I can't keep it," she said, with a hint of the emotion he

didn't see on her face. "I'm the one who—"

"It would have ended anyway." She looked startled at that, and he let out a small laugh. "Come on, Celia. You know it would have. In all the time we were engaged, you never set a date for the wedding. You kept changing the subject. And I hadn't been happy for a long time. We can stand here and blame you for it if you want, but that's not really fair. You gave us both a way out. You picked the guy I couldn't pretend I was okay with." He moved toward her then and closed her hand over the ring, accepting the bittersweet thing that worked in him then, like sorrow. But softer. "Keep it. I don't want it."

"Griffin—"

"Why don't you sit down?"

He moved to the sofa across from her and waited for her to ease herself down, like she was afraid either the pillows below her were breakable or she was. Maybe they both were, he thought. If he regretted anything, it was that he'd never understood that until now. She deserved better. But then, so did he.

"Don't worry," he said when he saw the expression on her face, the way she struggled to compose herself, "the hard part is over. This is about the business. And I think you're going to like what I have to say."

MARGERY'S WEDDING DAY dawned cold. Winter cold.

In the tradition of Montana's capricious springs, the

temperatures had plummeted with little warning the night before and the land glittered with an unexpected frost come the morning. Emmy had spent the night—the last two nights, in fact—sleeping on the couch in Gran Harriet's study with an inadequate selection of blankets, which meant she had a long stretch of peace and quiet, gazing out over the chilly land framed in Gran's huge central window and deliberately not thinking about a freaking thing, before she heard someone pad up beside her.

She knew it was Margery even before her sister sighed. She accepted the mug of coffee Margery handed to her and then they stood like that for a moment, their shoulders brushing and their eyes on the sweep of lawn out in front that rolled down toward the white tent on the bluff. Marietta looked small and cozy down below on the valley floor, with chimneys puffing out smoke here and there beneath clouds that Emmy wasn't going to point out looked a whole lot like snow.

"I suppose I had this coming," Margery said philosophically. "Mom told me to do this in August when we could be reasonably sure of the weather but I refused to get married in all that humidity. I didn't want to be sweating like a pig in all my photos. It never occurred to me I might have to wear a parka instead."

"On the bright side," Emmy pointed out, "you'll look particularly cute in a wedding dress with a parka on top."

"I certainly will," Margery said, a smile in her voice if not on her face. "Which is what matters."

"That and the love, of course."

Margery's shoulder pressed hers that little bit harder. "And that."

And Emmy decided she didn't have any time to think about that deep note of contentment in her sister's voice, or reflect on how little of that was likely to sound in her own, because there was a raucous family breakfast to sit through. Within an hour of her getting up there were cousins and aunts and uncles chattering in every available room. Guests stopped by to drop off gifts. Emmy took delivery of the flowers from the very nice Risa, the new owner of the florist's shop in town. She helped her mother put the final touches on the centerpieces and oversaw the placement of all those vanity chocolates in their pretty copper boxes.

She was already worn out when she retreated to the farthest reaches of the finished basement downstairs in search of a dog toy Gran Harriet was certain had been left there and needed immediately, for some reason, to find her father smoking one of the cigars he'd been supposed to give up years ago.

"Busted," she said.

Her father rolled his expressive eyes and blew a stream of smoke out of an open storm window.

"If a man can't have a cigar on his daughter's wedding day, when can he have one?"

"An argument you clearly didn't make with Mom or you

wouldn't be hiding in the basement," Emmy said dryly.

Her father only smiled. "Marriages are only strengthened by the secrets we pretend to keep," he said. "She will pretend not to smell my sin on my clothes and I'll pretend it didn't happen and this, my darling girl, is how we've remained together for thirty years."

"Lying?" She couldn't help herself, then. She thought that if lying was what it took for a happy marriage then Celia—the astoundingly attractive Celia, a small fact no one had mentioned—and Griffin must be destined for deep and abiding bliss, and it made her want to scream. Or break things. "And here I would have thought lying was a bad thing."

"Lying *is* a bad thing," her father said. "No one's lying. But the deliberate decision to choose *not* to bring up something that will only cause a fight? That's marital harmony right there. You'll see."

She decided not to tell him that she very much doubted she ever would.

Emmy had spent the past two days in a state of numbness. She'd walked out of the Italian restaurant in town after Celia's appearance and had found herself staring up blankly at St. James's Church while the spring evening stayed blue and bright—when all she wanted was to be hidden away in shadows. Hidden somewhere so far away that what had happened inside the restaurant couldn't touch her.

She'd found herself wandering the streets of Marietta like

this was some kind of country song, and had acted like she'd meant to be there when she'd run into some of her cousins outside of Gray's Saloon. She'd eaten dinner and smiled and drank a little too much beer, and then, when her cousins had dropped her off at the cabin, she'd sat on the couch in the great room and stared at all the places she and Griffin had come together.

It was going to be fine, she'd told herself. Griffin and Celia needed to talk about some things, obviously, but then he'd come home and they'd finish the conversation they'd started in the restaurant, and everything would be *fine*.

But when she'd woken up the following morning, her head had pounded and her mouth had been too dry. She was still on the couch, in a weird position that suggested she'd simply slumped to one side there, and she was still in the clothes she'd worn out the night before.

And Griffin wasn't there.

She'd packed up her things on autopilot, she'd stood in the shower and forced back all the memories of sharing it with him, and she'd told herself she should have known better. This was what he did. He always left when it would hurt her the most. Always. How had she managed to forget that?

She supposed she should count herself lucky that she'd actually left that restaurant last night still wearing her clothes.

Only when she'd realized that she was dawdling in his

kitchen, obviously killing time in the hope he'd turn up with explanations and declarations and all the rest of the things she'd imagined he'd do ten years ago, too, and he hadn't, had she forced herself to drive back over to Gran Harriet's in the ratty old car that she'd been borrowing this week, telling anyone who asked—and a few who hadn't—that she'd sleep here through the wedding, the better to be right on hand as maid of honor.

How thoughtful of you to be such a rock for your sister, Gran Harriet had said placidly, eyeing Emmy over the top of her Kindle screen.

I'm nothing if not thoughtful, Emmy had replied. Through her teeth.

She convinced herself that she was fine. She'd head home on Monday as planned and wasn't that great? She'd finally had a full-fledged fling. She'd finally burst out of her sheltered little bubble and lived a little. Surely all the strange things she was feeling was nothing more than joy. Pure, unadulterated, excruciatingly painful *joy.*

Even when Griffin had failed to show up for the Grans' party that next night, she didn't fall apart, or torture herself with a thousand images of what was very likely keeping him away.

Something came up with his business, his mother had said, not that Emmy had been loitering near the appetizers for the express purpose of eavesdropping on that conversation, because that would be crazy. *He's sorry to miss out, but he'll be here for the wedding on Saturday.*

Part of being as fine as she was, Emmy told herself, was that she *didn't* get as drunk as she wanted after hearing that and she *didn't* render herself paralytic when the day before the wedding dragged on by and he didn't so much as shoot her a text. No one else might realize the heroics involved in behaving as if she was the same old Emmy she'd always been, if dolled up in a bridesmaid's dress and wearing too much makeup, but she knew exactly how hard this was.

It sat in her stomach like lead.

She didn't see him at the ceremony, conducted on Gran Harriet's wide back stairs under hastily erected heat lamps in the biting cold, and she told herself she didn't look once. Or only looked once. She wore her dahlia-colored dress and she arranged Margery's train to look pretty and she smiled.

She smiled through the ceremony. She smiled while Margery and Philip kissed and everybody cheered. She smiled through all the interminable pictures and she sat at the high table and picked at her dinner and smiled all the more. She toasted her sister and made Margery teary in a good way, for once, and then the dancing started and it was time, she decided, to drink.

Heavily and plentifully. And if she started hitting on the groomsmen or woke up face down beneath one of the tables, oh well. No one could say she hadn't done her job as maid of honor first. She marched over to the caterer and liberated a bottle of white wine, and then she settled herself down in a far corner of the tent, where she could feel the wind from outside and where, if she was lucky, no one would see her become very, very drunk.

She tipped the bottle to her mouth and was about to take a long, hard swig when it was gently removed from her possession.

"Easy, killer. That's a nasty headache waiting to happen."

Griffin, of course. Because life was cruel and he was worse.

Emmy didn't want to look up at him, but she couldn't seem to help herself.

Shit, she thought helplessly as her eyes moved up over all of his magnificence packed tight into a perfectly fitted dark suit. Only the faintest hint of a tattoo poked out from the cuff of one sleeve, and on the back of his neck, and her curse was that it made her burn for him. His green eyes were brighter than she remembered and his muscles seemed harder and she wished she'd never heard of Griffin Hyatt. She wished she could reach inside her head and excise him, just like that.

Instead, she smiled, because they'd never promised each other anything and if he wanted to get back with his fiancée, he should. And because she'd been smiling all day long. What was one more?

"How's Celia?" she asked. "Did you all have fun catching up?"

"Yes," he said, the wine bottle dangling from one hand

and his gaze a hard thing on hers. "It was a delightful trip down memory lane. Because what's better than looking up from the woman you love to see the woman who left you?"

She couldn't possibly have heard that right.

"Yeah, that's what I said," he threw at her, a little belligerently, she thought. "I love you, Emmy. And I know you love me. You've loved me since you were a kid. You're ruined for all other men and I hope I haunt you forever, I really do."

"There's no need to be rude, Griffin," she snapped at him, shooting up to her feet, her hands on her hips before she knew she was moving. "What's the matter with you?"

"I can't stand you looking at me like that," he said quietly. Softly. Making her start to tremble way down deep inside. "Like I broke your heart all over again."

"Let's examine the facts," she said with a coolness she might have admired had her heart been capable of beating properly, instead of leaping all over the place inside of her like that. "I'm not saying my heart has anything to do with this conversation but if it did? It probably wouldn't have enjoyed you staring at your ex like she was the second coming before you disappeared—presumably with said ex—for two days. You own a company, Griffin. I've seen the computer equipment in your cabin and I've watched you take business calls. All of this suggests that if you wanted to talk to me, you would have. You didn't."

"I did." He reached over like he meant to trace her

mouth with his fingers but stopped, and Emmy thought that might hurt worse than all the rest of it. "I had to take care of a few things first."

"I got that part." She didn't even try to force a smile then. "Your silence was very loud, actually. A lot like it was ten years ago."

"I bought a shop," he said. Blurted out, really. "Down in town. I'm going to open a tattoo parlor. Just me, I mean. No GriffinFlight."

She blinked, and thinking about tattoos was easier than thinking about the crushed thing in her chest where her heart had been. "That's a great idea. But how will you run the company if you're tattooing people?"

"I'm selling it," he said, with a current of intensity in his voice and in his green eyes that she refused to let get to her. "That's what I've been doing for the past two days. I've been holed up in the Graff Hotel hammering it all out with my lawyers. Henry and Celia are going to run it. They're better at it anyway."

"Good." Her voice stuck somewhere in her throat, but she pushed it out. "I'm happy for you. All of you."

"I'm free, Emmy," he told her softly. "And the only thing I want that I don't already have is you."

For a second, then, Emmy let herself imagine that things might work out this time. That this wasn't ten years ago.

But there was no point making it easy on either one of them. "What makes you think you can have me?"

"You love me something crazy," he said, his mouth kicking up in one corner. "I thought we covered that."

"I have a crush on you, maybe. An infatuation that will surely fade and three weeks of okay sex."

He laughed. "If that's only 'okay,' I hope we never upgrade to good. We'll burn the town down."

She didn't want to hope, she thought then. It was too painful. She didn't dare. She'd tried to tell him she loved him in that restaurant and his ex had appeared, as if summoned. What would happen if she actually said it? Would Copper Mountain fall down on top of them?

"You're conceited and arrogant and you're not going to change. You've been exactly the same your entire life." She glared at him, because it was easier to do that than face all those dark, shadowy, fearful things inside of her. "I've gotten over you before, Griffin. It shouldn't be that hard to do it again."

He looked down at her for a long moment, while the band played something sweet. Inside her chest, Emmy's heart seemed to dance along with it, much less crushed and ruined than she'd thought it was only a few moments before. Or maybe that was the look in his eyes, making her forget she'd ever doubted him. Making her wonder how she ever could have.

Make her think it might be worth it to risk the mountain falling down, after all.

"Come here," he said. He reached over and took her

hand in his, and led her out of the tent and into the cool night air, and she went with him.

Of course she went with him.

It was the temperature that hit her first, that slap of winter and the immediate muffling of the sounds from within when the tent flap closed behind them. There were lanterns set up on metal posts, dotting the lawn and the path back up to Gran Harriet's house, which blazed with light at the crest of the hill.

And all around them, snow fell, a quiet dance from above.

Emmy couldn't help herself. She shivered. And not because she was cold. But she didn't complain when Griffin moved behind her and wrapped his arms around her, enveloping her in all of that heat and that scent of his, soap and man and *him*.

"I love you," he said, deeper somehow, out here where it was so quiet and there was nothing to distract from the power of it. No crowd this time. No interruptions. Only the snow above and the too-loud beating of her nervous heart. "I think I always have. It's snowing all over us, Bug, but as long as you're with me, it's summer. Don't you know that? We make it summer, you and me."

There wasn't much fight in her but she let out a sigh as if there was, leaning her head back against his shoulder, letting her cheek rest against his, and if it was still cold, she stopped noticing.

"This will never work. I'll uproot myself and move here, leaving everything I know in Atlanta—"

"Do you actually *like* Atlanta or do you not hate it? It's not the same thing."

"—and we'll have a great summer, but fall will come, and then the endless winter—"

"That happens. Every year. Don't forget the snow."

"—and we'll fight. And it will all go horribly wrong. And you'll still be Griffin Hyatt, who sold a company to open a tattoo parlor because he can do as he likes. While I'll be the idiot who stranded herself in Montana with some guy she should have gotten over when she was a teenager."

He laughed, and she found she was smiling when he turned her around in his arms and shook his head at her.

"Or," he said, truth and finality and a thousand shining things in his beautiful eyes, "you'll be the woman I love, and this will be our life, and we'll live happily ever after because guess what, Bug?"

"What?" But she was smiling up at him.

"You love me so much you can't see straight. You're not going anywhere. You're not getting over me and we're not breaking up no matter how much we fight. I'd marry you right now but it would upset your sister."

And she couldn't tell the difference between his smile and hers. As if they'd blended, somehow, out here in the cold night air.

"That and you should probably propose, first, and see

what I say. I could go either way. It might hinge on whether or not you need someone to run this tattoo shop of yours because I feel like I'd be excellent at bossing you around. And I want a salary. With benefits."

He bit at her neck, and she laughed, and there was nothing in the sound of it but joy. And this time, it didn't hurt one bit.

"There will be benefits." His kiss was hard and possessive, sweet and perfect, just like him. "Nothing but benefits, Emmy. That's the point."

"You're right," she whispered.

"About which part?"

"I love you," she told him, and the way he smiled then told her he wasn't quite as sure of himself as he pretended to be. It made her heart flip over and her smile that much wider. "I've always loved you. And I'll *consider* marrying you, but only under one condition."

"Name it."

She slid her hand over his heart and he covered it with his.

"It has to feel like this, Griffin," she whispered. "Always."

And she believed that it would, as he lifted her in his arms and spun her around. Around and around in their own wild dance, until they were both laughing with the sheer perfection of it.

Because it might get hard, as all things got hard. They might fight, and they might hurt each other, because that's what people in love did sometimes whether they wanted to do it or not. There would always be dark mixed in with the light, because that was the joy and the ache of living, but at the heart of it there would always be this. All the long, golden summers they carried between them and could take out when they wanted, just like this.

Even in the snow and the dark of night, they'd always have their summers, together.

INSIDE THE WEDDING tent, two very old friends sat next to each other in the padded, brocaded chairs Margery had insisted were necessary to her happiness and watched the dancers who covered the parquet floor before them.

And the couple who snuck out of the tent, about as secretive as a stampede of buffalo.

"You owe me fifty dollars, Martha," Gran Harriet said with great satisfaction. "I told you we'd end up related to each other, sooner or later."

"You were drinking too much wine and you had all the grandiose notions of the seventeen year old debutante you were," Gran Martha said with a snort from beside her. "I hardly think that counts."

"What counts is that I was right," Gran Harriet replied. "As I so often am. Pay up."

"So you were," Gran Martha said. She reached into her handbag and pulled out a crisp hundred-dollar bill and placed it on the table between them. Then she smiled blandly and tapped it with her index finger.

"Double or nothing," she said. "The first baby will be a girl, and they'll name her after me."

"Over my dead body." Gran Harriet bristled in feigned outrage. Well, partially feigned. "You'd better hope it's a boy."

"You're on," her best friend said, and they clinked their champagne glasses together and drank on it, the way they had a thousand years ago when they'd been so young and so silly they'd made up prophecies in their dormitory and called it fate.

And all around them, the party swirled on. The bride beamed with happiness, the groom was handsome and attentive, and the grandchildren they'd wanted together for a very long time now pushed back inside the tent, brimming with brand new promises and shining like love, dusted all over with springtime snow. Like a blessing.

Like it really was fate, after all.

THE END

If you enjoyed **A Game of Brides**, you will love these other Montana Born stories by Megan Crane!

Tempt Me, Cowboy

Please Me, Cowboy

Come Home for Christmas, Cowboy

In Bed with the Bachelor

Bad Boy Short Story

Project Virgin

Single Titles

I Love the 80s

Once More with Feeling

Available now at your favorite online retailer!

ABOUT THE AUTHOR

USA Today bestselling, RITA-nominated, and critically-acclaimed author **Megan Crane** has written more than fifty books since her debut in 2004. She has been published by a variety of publishers, including each of New York's Big Five. She's won fans with her women's fiction, chick lit, and work-for-hire young adult novels as well as with the Harlequin Presents she writes as **Caitlin Crews**. These days her focus is on contemporary romance from small town to international glamor, cowboys to bikers, and beyond. She sometimes teaches creative writing classes both online at mediabistro.com and at UCLA Extension's prestigious Writers' Program, where she finally utilizes the MA and PhD in English Literature she received from the University of York in York, England. She currently lives in the Pacific Northwest with a husband who draws comics and animation storyboards and their menagerie of ridiculous animals.

Visit Megan at www.megancrane.com.

Thank you for reading

A Game of Brides

If you enjoyed this book, you can find more from all our great authors at TulePublishing.com, or from your favorite online retailer.

TULE
PUBLISHING

Made in United States
Troutdale, OR
12/10/2024